I0819910

LOVE SONGS WHILE HEARTBROKEN

A COLLECTION OF SHORT STORIES

KIA SMITH

Kia Smith Writes

DEDICATION

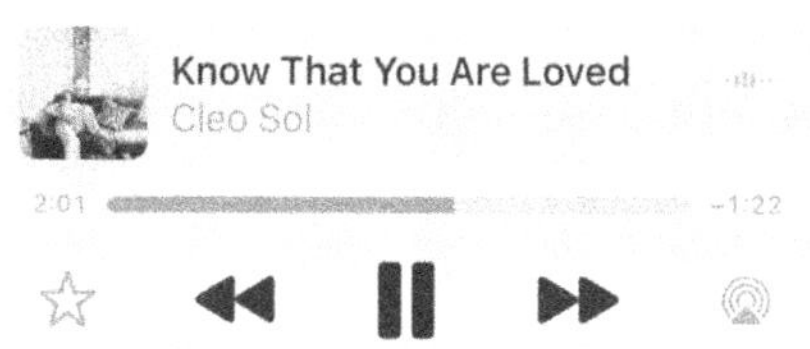

To the bad bitches, the drama queens, the lover girls... the ones they said feel too much and love too deeply.

Know that you are enough.

Play Cleo Sol – Know That You Are Loved when you forget.

AUTHOR'S NOTE

A few years ago, I went through what felt like my worst heartbreak. Astonishingly, my zest for being creative overflowed, and from there, I birthed all these stories.
What inspired these stories? The answer is heartbreak.
Some are just fragments of my imagination, torn from journals and the Notes app on my phone.

All standalones.

All of these are very short, and some are not fully fleshed out, with no intention to expound upon them, but who knows what the future holds? ;)
Though not heartbroken anymore, I honor the season I was in that allowed me to fall back in love with writing — the one thing that fixed my broken heart. The other thing that fixed my broken heart was music. In this book, you'll see some mentions of songs that got me through one of my darkest, confusing, and most heart-wrenching times. When the words escaped me, these artists and their art filled in the gaps. You can find the full soundtrack to each story in the playlist section, both for Apple Music and Spotify.

At the beginning of writing these stories, I hoped that by reading these, then maybe, just *maybe,* it could fix your broken heart too. The more I wrote, the more I realized that fixing the broken heart isn't the goal.... Maybe you'll walk away feeling seen, heard, and understood. At the very least, maybe you'll walk away feeling entertained.

But as long as you feel *something*, then my job is done.

P.S. – A common theme in this collection of shorts is heartbreak: the good, the bad, the ugly, and how you overcome. There are no happily ever afters in this book. I understand that this topic may not be everyone's cup of tea. There are other things in my catalog that you can read if you don't want to be reminded of the time(s) you were sliding down the wall like Summer Walker.

Happy Reading!
XOXO,
Kia

FOR YOUR LISTENING PLEASURE

Of course I made a playlist. Click the links below:

Apple

Spotify

Before You Walk Out My Life

PART I

BEFORE YOU WALK OUT MY LIFE

1

The vibes were awkward between Wynter and Onyx. Though they had broken up over a year ago, it was hard to forget everything that had happened between them, much less have a separation between them.

For 365 days, Wynter picked up the pieces of her broken heart and rebuilt a life without Onyx the best way that she knew how. Getting a master's degree, moving to downtown Atlanta, and planning on opening up her own Urban Fiction bookstore, Wynter was busy for sure... but she was lonely. She thought Onyx would be the man she married and had babies with. They were building a life together, and their lives were intricately intertwined. Yes, they were individuals, but at the end of the day, it was them against the world.

Unfortunately, everything was different. And while Wynter was proud of the progress she'd made, she wondered when the aching feeling of having no one to share it with would go away.

"This is fuckin' stupid," Wynter grumbled to herself as she stared out the plane's window. Back in Atlanta, she barely had time to sit down and threw herself into school and work to distract herself from her broken heart. Here, on the two-hour flight back home to Chicago,

Wynter had too much time to think about her old life. The only reason she was coming back was for her best friend Cali's birthday.

She couldn't help but think how a year ago, it was her, Cali, Onyx, and Cali's man, Indigo, all in Dubai celebrating Cali's birthday. Those five days were part birthday celebration, part group baecation.

It was blissful.

It was beautiful.

It was fun.

And now, it was absolutely nothing between them.

2

E*very nigga gotta make decisions and stand on the ones he makes. Cuz if you don't wanna stand on it, then you shouldn't be out here doing shit that'll have you making hard decisions.*

That was the first thing that popped into Onyx's mind when he woke up early Saturday morning. Running his hand through his beard, his eyes popped open, and instinctively, he reached over to the spot where Wynter used to lay, before realizing that she was gone.

And she had been gone for over a year now.

Dread settled in. Yeah, he fucked up, but he missed Wynter. But his infidelity and betrayal made her not ever wanna fuck with him again.

He scoffed at the thought, but he understood it... Wynter was as loyal as they come. If you looked up the definition, her picture should be next to it. You couldn't play with her if you tried, and after her fair share of heartbreaks before Onyx, she vowed very early on to cut off anyone who decided to play with her, *even if* she loved them. Despite her quiet and rigid exterior, Wynter was a lover girl at her core, and Onyx missed the way she loved him.

She was an intentional lover, her aura magnetic and electrifying all at once.

She was the perfect combination of brains, beauty, and booty.

She was in his corner when no one else was, and she inspired him to want to be a better man.

But as natural human nature would have it, Onyx made the decision that only an emotionally immature man would make, and that decision cost him Wynter.

As audacious as it sounded, her walking away from him fucked with him. Not that he underestimated her... okay, maybe he did. But, he thought her love for him would make her more forgiving of his shortcomings.

How could someone be so fiery, yet calm and peaceful at the same time?

He brought out a softness in her that many were not privy to, *and* he never thought that softness would be traded for wrath meant for him and only him.

As much as he hated to admit it, though, he deserved her wrath.

Wynter wasn't a confusing woman. In fact, she made things extremely clear when they got together and throughout their three-year relationship.

"I'll love you with everything in me, but if you ever cross me, I'll act as if you never existed," she warned him once over dinner. Her tone was measured and even, while her beautiful brown eyes bore into him.

Onyx made promises that night that he failed to live up to years later.

Those eyes..

Onyx let out a sigh so deep that he was sure the neighbors next door heard him when he thought about those eyes. Wynter's eyes were a beautiful shade of dark brown that twinkled golden when sunlight hit. They used to hold truth, power, and love in them for him. And when he broke her heart, they turned lifeless and cold, holding only rage, hurt, and contempt.

FULLY AWAKE AND sitting upright in his bed, he scrolled through his call log and then through his Instagram, his inbox filled with fine women wanting a shot at him. Being back on the market as a single man had many women wanting him, and while he indulged... Onyx was lonely without Wynter. She understood him in ways that his own family didn't, and she just didn't care about the superficial stuff.

Many flocked to Onyx because he was a popular artist and not ugly at all. Standing over six feet tall with a muscular build and obsidian colored skin with a full beard, he matched his physical attributes with charisma and charm. Pair that with dressing nice and the ability to sing a bitch right out of her panties, he got attention wherever he went and often basked in it, because what nigga didn't love attention?

Wynter was different, though. She was his turn-up buddy, his trusted confidant, his consultant, and a great listener. She was truly someone who believed in all his dreams, no matter if they sounded silly to someone else. For every show he had, she was either backstage or front row and right next to him at every club appearance he had to make. She spent hours in the studio with him and always gave her honest opinion on songs. Wynter brought out the best in him, and he fumbled her.

Onyx shook his head. He hadn't seen nor heard from Wynter in over a year. When they broke up, she blocked him from everything and shortly after, moved out of state. The only time he saw how she was doing was when he looked on his best friend — more like a little sister — Cali's page, who was best friends with Wynter.

And as time would have it, she looked good and seemed to be doing even better. The thought pissed Onyx off, but he quickly doused the fire that was rising within him. Wynter deserved to be happy after everything he put her through. So even though he wasn't ready, he was looking forward to laying eyes on Wynter at Cali's birthday party.

3

"Bitch, you look gooooood!' Cali exclaimed, smacking Wynter quickly on the asss as she walked past her to look in the mirror one last time.

Cali was having an intimate birthday dinner at her Uncle Smoke's new restaurant and Wynter would not have missed her bestie's birthday for anything in the world. Life in Atlanta was lonely, so Wynter took the chance to see Cali whenever she could.

This birthday was no different, even with thousands of miles between them now.

Wynter laughed at Cali's antics and sized herself up in the mirror. Always a petite girl, Wynter stood tall at only five feet three with smooth brown skin that tanned a beautiful shade of dark chocolate in the summer months. Cali requested that all her guests wear either emerald green or burnt orange, so Wynter opted for an emerald green dress that was sparkly and short. Though she lost the weight she gained when she was in her relationship, she kept her body nice and toned with a combo of pilates, dance, and daily walks in Atlanta. The results made her dress look painted on, while a pair of burnt orange heels gave her extra height, completing the look. Her ginger colored faux locs were pulled into an intricate bun, and her makeup was flawless, neutral, and soft with green and orange eye shadow popped in the corner of her lids, accentuating those pretty brown eyes. Other than birthdays, Wynter loved getting dressed and putting her shit on. In Wynter's mind, every day was an occasion, and ever since she was a young girl, it was instilled in her to look interesting wherever she went.

Cali was no different. Her all white, diamond and silk-encrusted gown with iridescent green and burnt orange jewels that adorned her tall, model-esque body was a showstopper. Those who knew and loved Cali expected nothing less from the birthday girl. She commanded attention no matter where she went and rocked pieces from her boutique almost daily. Cali was a fashionista through and through and wore shit no one would ever think of.

The pair snapped it up both in the mirror on their phones and with the photographer she had hired for the night before leaving for dinner.

HOPPING IN THE BLACK TRUCK, the ladies took the thirty-minute drive feeling good and looking better, until Wynter got quiet.

"You aight over there?" Cali asked, taking a moment to pause from responding to her birthday messages.

"I'm cool. You cool?" Wynter deflected. She knew what Cali was really asking, but she didn't want to talk about her feelings tonight. On the outside, it seemed like Wynter was a woman who moved on effortlessly. She bossed up and would continue bossing up, with or without a nigga.

On the inside, she was still torn up about her breakup. She wasn't sure if she missed Onyx or if she simply missed the comfort that her old life provided her, but heartbreak on top of loneliness in a new city made her stomach hurt. She spent many nights crying, and while most women just filled their voids by getting under a new man,

Wynter filled it with school and opening her business. Truth be told, she didn't want to entertain anyone new because she was terrified of getting played again.

She had one rule when it came to being with her, and that was: don't play with her. The moment you played, she would be unforgiving, depending on the offense, and Onyx's betrayal immediately crossed the line. Her therapist wanted her to explore whether or not her boundaries were too rigid, but Wynter refused. As soon as she caught wind of Onyx's infidelity, he was cut like a terrible athlete. He couldn't even sit on her bench; he was exiled from the whole league. The only reason she accepted the friendship between Cali and Onyx was because they were close like family, and in a strange way, they needed each other. Despite the awkwardness of it all, in true Wynter fashion, she laid down some very clear boundaries:

- *Block Onyx on everything*
- *Make Cali swear not to talk to her about him.*
- *Don't bring him up to Cali either*

Cali agreed and stuck to her word. What Wynter didn't know was that Onyx asked about Wynter every so often, but she was tight-lipped, often changing the subject. While Cali loved him like a brother, their relationship wouldn't exist without Wynter, so the loyalty and alliance swung more in her favor. Wynter was her best friend since high school, and she knew how she didn't fuck around when it came to her boundaries. So, she kept quiet. In Cali's eyes, right was right, and wrong was wrong. She did her best to stay neutral, but she was riding for her sister every time. Wynter wasn't the type to let many see her cry, but she knew their breakup was serious business when she had to pick up Wynter and sit with her many times to get through her transition period of heartbreak. While planning her birthday this year, Cali asked her numerous times if she was cool with Onyx coming to the dinner, to which she replied, *"Girl, it's your day. Do whatever you want,"* before changing the subject.

Wynter was uncomfortable with the idea of people accommodating her because of her breakup. She didn't want to seem weak or disrupt anyone else's normal, so if she had to grin and bear it for her best friend's birthday dinner, then that's what she would do.

Cali took another look at her and asked her again if she was good. Wynter confirmed that she was, and as the truck lulled to a stop in front of the venue, Wynter's stomach dropped to her toes. Hand in hand, Wynter and Cali entered the venue where the party was awaiting.

4

Onyx was already there, waiting with the rest of the guests for Cali's entrance.

He looked good, with a fresh cut and a burnt orange colored satin suit with emerald green pocket squares and a white V-neck shirt. Dark shades adorned his face and concealed his eyes. With the shades on, he was also to observe everybody and hide his true self at the same time.

While Cali didn't confirm, he knew that Wynter would be there because that was her best friend. She never missed a birthday. And with this being his first time seeing her in person since the breakup, he was nervous.

Would she say something to him?

Would she ignore him?

Would she slap him?

Should he say something to her?

His thoughts were interrupted by a cute woman, who happened to recognize him from his latest music video. Her mouth was running a mile a minute, and while he liked the attention, her words were going in one ear and out the other, as he tried to catch a glimpse of Wynter when she walked through the door.

"So, your number?" the attractive woman asked, snapping him back to the present. Onyx paused. The girl was cute, but he was not interested at the moment.

Before he got a chance to politely decline her, the crowd turned towards the entry where Afrobeat music started playing, and about fifteen men and women did a dance routine dressed in African attire. It was a sight to see and borrowed straight from *Coming To America.* Cali gracefully walked over the green and orange rose petals, smiling for the cameras and hugging every guest as they cheered on.

Onyx was happy to see Cali, but his eyes panned to the only woman he could say had stolen his heart. She was slimmer now, but he knew those legs, that skin, and her aura anywhere. He inhaled deeply, hoping to catch a whiff of her signature scent: brown sugar with a hint of something fresh. He heard her laugh and realized that it was something he missed hearing. Wynter had the type of laugh that, when you heard it, made you want to laugh too. His laughs these days were hollow and didn't come from his belly like they did when he was with her. His life had been reduced to fake smiles and keeping up an image, and on many of his nights, he used liquor, weed, and pointless sex to distract him from the emptiness he felt.

"Ummm... rude much?" Little Miss Groupie's voice cut through his observation, and he felt bad that she was still there. Wynter would've never hung around in a nigga's face when it was clear that his attention was elsewhere. He remembered when they would cuddle up in bed, laughing at the girls in his message requests who offered him every dollar in their accounts to their unborn children just to get close to him.

"These hoes ain't got no decorum!" Wynter would cackle, with tears in her eyes at how thirsty they were being. Everyone knew who had Onyx's heart and soul. He dedicated a whole album to her and posted her all over his page. He respected her in public and in private... until one slip-up. One err in his judgement...

One thing that he would regret forever.

Onyx sighed and looked down at the woman, eagerness shining all through her eyes.

"Unfortunately... I'm spoken for," he lied. The groupie's eyes fell, and she nodded politely, lips in a thin line. Onyx wasn't one to be overtly rude to women — his reputation was already questionable once they got word of what he did to Wynter. So he didn't need any questionable interactions with women that could potentially be brought to a gossip blog. Once the groupie slipped away, he looked around the room, and like a magnet, his eyes landed on Wynter.

She looked hypnotizing. So much so that, to Wynter's sheer horror, Onyx crossed the room and was now standing directly in front of her.

5

Wynter was always able to *feel* Onyx. They once shared a love that made her want to search for him with a flash-light in the daytime. So it was no surprise that she felt his piercing eyes on her, albeit covered by his shades. It had been a while, but no matter what rooms they were in, his eyes would always find her.

"Wassup y'all?" he greeted Cali's Uncle Smoke and one of her cousins. They nodded at him and dapped him up, unaware that Wynter was about to start hyperventilating. Sucking in a breath didn't help because all she caught was his delightful-smelling cologne that used to make her cream instantly. To steady herself, Wynter put some space between them, but all that made Onyx do was subtly move closer to her. Discreetly, her eyes flashed at him in anger, but Onyx knew she wouldn't cut up.

Wynter hated scenes.

And she definitely wouldn't cause one in the middle of her best friend's birthday dinner party.

Onyx watched her face flash with a smile that didn't reach her eyes, and he gulped. Maybe she changed... maybe she was about to cut into him with her words.... maybe —

"Onyx. Step outside with me real quick," her voice came out low, measured, with an iciness to it that was synonymous with her name.

But… at least she was talking to him.

It'd been so long since he heard her voice in any capacity, and he missed it.

Everything about her.

So he obliged, knowing that he wasn't prepared for the verbal spar that she would inflict upon him. In his mind, if her words pierced him in the ways that bullets do, then that meant she still cared for him.

And Wynter still caring, felt better than the cold front she left behind.

6

Whoever said that love didn't hurt was a fuckin' liar. And more than anything, Wynter hated liars.

Love hurt.

It cracked you open, right down the middle and left you bleeding out, screaming to the top of your lungs and nobody heard you. Nobody stopped to make sure you were okay. Some even felt like you deserved the hurt.

But Wynter didn't deserve this.

She didn't want to look at someone she once loved with so much contempt and disgust now. She was confused — because her heart ached and the cause and cure was staring at her in her face, chewing on his bottom lip, waiting on her to say something. Venomous words were at the tip of her tongue. She imagined for 365 days straight what she would say to him if he they ever crossed paths again. But now here he was, in the flesh, looking good in his satin suit and her levees almost broke.

People don't talk about how the other side of heartbreak is grief. Endless, repetitive, aching grief. She had her *Cranes in The Sky* ass moment — she tried to drink it away, smoke it away, shop it away, move thousands of miles away.. but no matter what she did, she couldn't outrun grief. Grief cuddled with her at night and taunted her during the day. Running didn't work but absorbing herself in it damn near killed her.

"You look beautiful, Wyn" Onyx broke the ice but not the one around her heart.

She blinked at him.

Once.

Twice.

Three times.

Time stood still and Onyx wanted to engulf her in a hug but knew she didn't want him touching her. He searched her eyes for a flicker of hope, but instead her eyes were filled with dread. Onyx wanted to kick his own ass for this half-ass plan, but he didn't... couldn't back down now.

Wynter didn't fuck with him anymore and it crushed him.

And he had no one to blame but himself for how cold she was being towards him. Audacity should've been his middle name because in spite of the tension, he smiled cautiously at her, pretending like he had everything under control.

"Onyx... I can't do this," Wynter shook her head and turned on her stiletto clad heel to walk back into the party. She didn't know who she was fooling but there was no way that she could stand to have a civil conversation with her ex.

They weren't buddies.

They didn't part ways amicably.

No, he betrayed her. There was evidence of his transgressions and that's what hurt even more than the act itself sometimes. Because sometimes, women who vibrated lower than she did took pride in another woman's tears. Their trophies were fucking someone else's man and instead of being discreet about it, they had to let the world know in 4K.

"Then when can we, Wyn? It's been colder than your name without you and you won't even let me apologize," Onyx spoke with urgency, an edge to his voice that broke his cool boy facade.

He was never too cool for school when it came to Wynter.

That girl *knew* him.

All of him.

And loved him anyway.

Not being with her was the equivalent of the earth not feeling the sun. Ongoing seasonal depression that couldn't be cured with vitamins, therapy, and occasional celibate periods.

Turning around slowly, he saw the conflict in her eyes.

She used to be so *sure* about him. Now she wasn't.

And that gutted him.

She sucked in a breath. "You don't... You don't get to ask me that, Onyx. Not here, *especially* not now... Not *never*, the fuck?!" her voice didn't shake. Wynter was the type of woman who meant what she said and said what she meant.

But still... Onyx had to try.

"Wynter... look at me," he commanded, stepping closer to her. She shut her eyes, squeezing them tightly... her worst nightmare had come true. That the cause and cure for her heartache stood right in front of her face and was demanding that she hear him out when her ears stopped working over a year ago. Her heart didn't beat the same, and her smile didn't always reach her eyes anymore, but there was nothing wrong with her life in Atlanta.... although she was almost crippled by the loneliness.

It was just grief.

And sometimes grief fought like hell to consume you, but Wynter wasn't the type to let it make her surrender. She fought back... but sometimes grief just fought harder. Sometimes it knocked her out. Sometimes it hurts. Sometimes it lingered and wore out its welcome.

"Onyx... *No.* Please, Cali's party is not the place for this shit. Just let it go. It's been a year. What more do you have to say? The damage is done." Wynter's eyes got glassy as she narrowed them, but he knew that she wouldn't mess up her perfectly applied makeup.

Onyx sighed, slumping his shoulders as they stared at one

another. Just as he was about to get on his knees and beg, Wynter opened her mouth again.

"You know... You just don't fuckin' get it," her voice dripped with venom as she wryly laughed. Onyx's heart stilled as he prepared himself for a long-overdue verbal lashing.

"For 365 days, I dreamed about what I would say to you if we ever crossed paths again. I rehearsed my lines a thousand times like that old Patty LaBelle song used to say..., but now that I stand in front of you, nothing I had rehearsed would actually suffice."

They turned their heads slightly, watching a car roll down the street, blasting that old Monica song with her crooning about how someone was walking out of her life. Wynter turned back to him, licked her lips, and finished speaking.

"I thought I would curse you out. Call you out your name.... humiliate you like your actions humiliated me... but that's not what I wanna do. I'm not happy to see you, but I'm not totally against it either—"

Onyx's brows raised in curiosity. Wynter had never been a woman who had conflicting and confused emotions. Onyx wondered, was it him who did this to her? Did he turn her into a woman who questioned herself? Did he make her into a woman who was unsure? The realization that he could have possibly ruined her hit him in the chest like a ton of bricks.

Wynter eyed him up and down, her orbs still glassy but too stubborn to let a tear fall. He wanted nothing more than to engulf her in a hug and kiss her tears away. He wanted nothing more than to let her know that despite his fuck up, he had learned and that she was still safe with him. He wanted to let her know that, despite her not trusting him, he would do everything in his power to show her that she still could.

But Wynter was stubborn.

Cross her once, you'd better hope to die. The cold shoulder she gave would make you wish you were dead anyway.

"Wynter... baby... I—" Onyx started, but Wynter held her hand up.

"I don't wanna hear you apologize, Onyx. I don't wanna hear you plead your case. I don't wanna hear how ole girl didn't mean anything to you and how that was your first and only fuck up. It was one fuck up too many...especially knowing how dirty my ex did me, Onyx... just never thought you would do me worse."

It got so quiet that you could hear a mouse piss on cotton. Onyx retreated within himself because every word out of her mouth was true. Onyx was very aware of how her ex, before him, treated her. As a result, Wynter was always very clear about what she would and would not accept. She wasn't super strict, but she was firm. She used to be very sure of herself.

And Onyx... Onyx was just a man. He thought he had a lot of self-control until that one stupid night showed that he didn't have as much control as he thought. Before that night, he wasn't presented with a lot of opportunities to lose control. Then it all changed. That decision caused him to lose the love of a lifetime.

This time, when Wynter turned on her heel to leave, he didn't stop her... and although she expressed the opposite, Wynter secretly expected him to. It shocked her, then saddened her when he didn't.

Maybe Tina Turner was right... Love ain't have much to do with anything.

As Onyx watched her leave, it felt like the other piece of his heart was taken with him, and maybe he needed to call Omarion up for an *Ice Box* remix.

The love of his life was gone for good, and sadly, there was nothing he could do about it. Instead of going back into Cali's party, he sauntered defeatedly to his car and ordered his driver to take him straight to the studio.

The End

You Know Him?

PART II

YOU KNOW HIM?

1

"You know him?"

Her world paused, if only for a millisecond.

Yeah, she knew him.

At least, at a point, she did.

How could she explain that she spent ten years of her life with him?

How could she explain that she worked seven years of her life by his side?

How could she explain that every single milestone in her 20s, he was right there?

How could she explain the losses? The gains? The wins? The struggles?

Serenity was her girl, but she didn't know the former her.

The one who loved a man with her entire heart.

The one who would give you the shirt off her back.

The one who only saw a future with him.

The one who —

"Tri? You heard me? I'm trying to book this new guy. Wanted to know if you know him. He's from your city," Serenity interrupted her fleeting thoughts. Just seeing his picture on the phone screen catapulted her to a time and space where she wasn't living in LA, wasn't a single woman, and she didn't have the new life that she created for herself.

To Tri, Serenity was lucky.

She was married to her college sweetheart, and they had two beautiful kids. Her husband was supportive and actually did his part as a husband and father. Serenity was a boss at the record label, but around her husband, she was able to turn her brain off. She was able to live the epitome of a soft life. She excelled in business, marriage, and motherhood.

She never knew what it was like to grieve someone who wasn't actually dead.

She never knew what it was like to walk away from all that was comfortable and familiar because, for some reason, God said that the people you love the most couldn't come with you to the next level.

She never knew what it was like to have that yearning still and grieve when certain dates passed.

Serenity had never known heartbreak like Tri knew heartbreak.

Tri hid that from her.

She poured herself all into work.

She had friends.

She had a successful career.

She had every material thing that she could imagine, but something was missing.

She spent the last five years alone.

Sometimes feeling lonely.

Sometimes feeling nothing.

She didn't keep up with too many people back home. It was a painful reminder that life, indeed, goes on. And so that meant that she had to put one Brandon Blackwood heel in front of the other and move on too.

And while it wasn't with another person per se,

She did move on in thought.

In wisdom.

In accomplishments.

In mindset.

Contrary to popular belief, she wasn't stuck in a time loop of the past. She elevated. She got serious about cultivating her own joy. She had hobbies. She went to church. She volunteered. She had successfully entered a new chapter.

But still... the reality of it all was jarring for Tri.

Grief was cruel like that.

Like on the day in March when they decided to make it their anniversary, she might feel nothing. But then, on the other hand, a random day like the 22nd of December, she might remember their first baecation to Puerto Rico.

But... she buried those emotions. After five years, she felt as if she should be over it and possibly in another relationship by now, but God clearly had jokes. Meanwhile, last she heard, ole boy was married with a kid on the way.

She stopped lurking on his social media in year one of the breakup and started limiting her own social media usage by year three.

So truthfully? She didn't know him anymore. He was a familiar stranger now. Nothing more, nothing less.

But the thought still gutted her.

Tri looked over at Serenity and squinted to buy herself more time.

"Ehhh. He looks familiar, but I'm not sure. He looks like he might be around my brother's age," Tri smoothly lied. Or was it really?

Because he looked the same but a little different. Time had been kind to him. She could tell from the picture that he had been in the gym by his arms. His beard was full and moisturized. He had new tattoos. His style was different, too. He used to only rock Jordan's exclusively, but now he was in Adidas. Tri wondered what sparked the change.

Swiping a piece of hair behind her ear and pushing her glasses up, Serenity glanced at Tri and then back to her phone screen before saying, "Hmmm. See what you can find on him. I think he'd be a great addition to our R&B roster and lord knows we need new faces since Sun's dumb ass got caught up in all that legal trouble."

Tri swallowed.

It felt like someone turned the thermostat up to hell.

Nodding, Tri responded, "Yeah, give me a day or two. I'll make some calls back home," and cringed inwardly.

Tri wasn't ready to see him after all these years, but she had a job to do. She finished her work day silently, crawling the internet for any piece of information she could find on Sir39, his R&B moniker. She simply knew him as Cee Jay Johnson, her former homie, lover, and friend.

Do you know him? Echoed in her mind as she walked into the parking lot.

I used to, she thought somberly to herself.

The End

Get Yo Lick Back

PART III

GET YO LICK BACK

1

"Would the accused like to make a statement?"

Azima rolled her shoulders back and stared blankly at the crowd before her. Her public defender looked nervous, and inwardly, Azima smiled. She was absolutely guilty of the crime she was accused of. Vengeance was hers, and she succeeded in what she set out to do. Her public defender begged her to plead temporary insanity.

To cop a plea.

To plead not guilty.

But the thing is, Azima didn't feel bad for what she did. She felt bad for her former self, who loved the two people closest to her, who betrayed her the most.

Azima's public defender cleared his throat, his pale skin and brunette hair sticking up every which way. He was young, fresh out of law school, and didn't have much experience in taking a case like hers.

It was exactly what Azima wanted. Inwardly, she smiled. She knew America took pity on her. A woman scorned, they had marked her but they had it all wrong.

Yes, her motivations to get her lick back were powered by the scorn after she discovered the betrayal.

Yes, she took it way too far.

Yes, she purposely got caught.

But no, they didn't need to feel sorry for her.

Azima McKnight didn't need anyone's *pity.*

What she *needed* was for people to take heed. To pay attention. And to never underestimate her kind heart again.

Slowly, Azima stood to her full height of five feet seven inches. Her red fitted skirt accentuated her hips and hit right at her knees, with a matching blood red blazer draped over her shoulders. An ear-length, bone straight, jet black, blunt cut bob wig adorned her head. Blood red lips. Perfume that had her smelling like money.

She sauntered confidently to the stand, keeping her expression neutral, and swore to tell the truth, the whole truth, and nothing but the truth.

Her palms were face down and she stared at the sea of faces that made up the audience. Low murmurs resounded around the courtroom, people judging her for her actions.

"Miss McKnight, how do you plead?" began the prosecuting attorney.

"Objection!" —— her public defender meekly croaked out, and it took everything for her eyes not to roll. Leaning forward, she put her lips to the mic and made eye contact with the one woman who used to mean the most to her.

"It's alright. I'll be swift," she started. Butterflies flew around in her stomach, but Azima ignored the sensation. Now was not the time to transform back into the meek girl she used to be. She made everyone else stand on business for what they did to her, and now it was time for her to stand on business about herself.

"I used to be a woman who let everyone play in her face. I wouldn't speak up. I would always try to keep the peace. I gave all I could until I had nothing left. I poured into the people I loved, even when my cup was empty. I used to think that if I was more selfless, more lenient, more loving.... that the people I loved would love me back. And for a while, it worked. I had a best friend. I had a man that I thought I would spend the rest of my life with. I finally had everything I worked so hard for. I was the perfect partner and the perfect friend.... Until I realized something," she paused after the last statement, looking each and every person in her close proximity in their eyes. Her days as a theater kid were paying off today.

"I realized... that none of it was enough. That you can do and be everything to some people, and it still won't make them love you. It won't make them respect you. And it sure as hell won't make them choose you, " she chuckled wryly, the weight of her words sinking in. Every woman and even some men in there knew exactly what she meant. They knew that overextending yourself, pretending to be cool with things you weren't cool with, and letting niggas and bitches walk all over you didn't yield any trophies or awards. No, you'd be blamed for being a human who simply wanted to love and be loved in return.

Azima realized it too late, after twenty-eight years of doing the same thing over and over again with the same results. She started to believe that she was asking for too much and settled for crumbs. She vented to her best friend, crying endlessly about how she wished things were different. How she felt like a prisoner to love. How she felt like her love was slipping away from her. How she'd do anything to keep him.

"Have you tried a threesome?" her "friend" asked, rubbing circles into her back one evening as Azima came crying her eyes out over the fact that her man was acting distant once again.

Azima's head snapped up. She wasn't attracted to women sexually, and she didn't care to share her man — or herself — with anyone. She respected those who engaged in that type of behavior, but certain things just wasn't for her. Then the doubt began to set in.

Was she not adventurous enough?

Was her nigga actually bored with her?

Could that be the reason he was distant?

AZIMA SNAPPED back from her walk down memory lane and made her final statement.

"The realization that I would never be enough for two people who didn't choose me anyway hit me like a ton of bricks. So yes... I let my anger and rage turn me into someone unrecognizable. But let me ask you this court..." Azima sat up straight, noticing how everyone's eyes were captivated by her speech.

"When betrayal comes from those closest to you, will you let go and let God, or will you dance with the devil to get your lick back too?"

Gasps echoed through the courtroom while Azima was escorted off the stand. The rest of the hearing passed in a blur, and soon, Azima was handcuffed, her public defender looking defeated, but inwardly, Azima smiled again. She already completed phase one.... now it was on to phase two of getting her lick back.

2

Azima was always an observant child. The only child from her mother, she watched her mother cook, clean, and wash everything while bearing a grin. Her father worked hard, paid all the bills, and tended to... female company outside of the home.

That couldn't be right, she often thought to herself. But, her mother stayed.

Cooking.

Cleaning.

Washing.

Grinning.

Bearing.

Like a bad rinse and repeat cycle, she watched her mother do it for twenty-one years of her life, until she passed away from ovarian cancer that no one knew she had, until Azima got a call from the doctor who was secretly treating her.

Her father seemingly disappeared off the face of the earth, starting a new life with her mother's best friend shortly after the funeral. Azima's life seemed like a lonely soap opera because though she attended the prestigious St. Holly University and was at the top of her classes, she was drowning on the inside.

Then she met Makeem Harris, who was as strong and as firm as the meaning of his name. They had a random sociology elective together. Random for him, as a University Studies major, but on track for her, as a future forensic psychologist. She was obsessed with *Law and Order: SVU* and wanted to get into the mind of criminals and solve the clusterfuck of crimes they commited. She always wondered things about people, like...

What made them stay in unhappy situations?

What made them tolerate more than they should?

What made them bear and grin when they really wanted to scream and shout?

And ultimately, what made them snap and seek revenge?

Human behavior fascinated her. Makeem Harris fascinated her even more.

She fell first. Azima was beautiful, but mousy. Meek and even-tempered, and slightly socially awkward, as she liked to make people think. She was never the loudest in the room or ever had the most to say. She became even more of a recluse when her mother died her junior year.

But Makeem Harris... he gave her a reason to enjoy life again. She'd had boyfriends before, in high school and the such, so she wasn't completely inexperienced. She'd been kissed, fucked, loved... but never really honored, cherished, or adored.

Until Makeem. The star quarterback studying University Studies whose pro football dreams were cut short by an achilles tendon injury that took a while to heal.

She observed him first, angry and annoyed at the world but not really trying to do much to change his situation. He came from a family that had old money, where his mom once served as the chancellor of St. Holly University and his father was a mysterious oil tycoon. Makeem walked – well, limped with an aura that was haughty. He knew he was the shit even if his dreams may have been deferred. A whole six weeks in the semester went by and he still hadn't said a word to her. Azima was perplexed by her crush on him. Yes, he was handsome with his wavy black hair, skin the color of a good gumbo roux, and minimal facial hair with golden brown eyes and a football player build. Yes, he drove a matte black Benz to campus and a different flavor of the week would walk him to class as if he was incapable.

And yes, she could confirm that he had a big dick that he knew how to use, because a sex tape of him digging some professor out was mysteriously air dropped on all the phones and computers that were compatible a few weeks ago.

The professor got fired.

Makeem had some extra pep in his step when he bopped into class the next morning.

"Azima McKnight! Makeem Harris! You two will be partners for the final project. Please govern yourselves accordingly," their professor called out. Azima turned behind her, where Makeem looked bored.

It's now or never, she thought to herself. Tucking her shoulder-length silk press behind her ear, she stood on shaky legs and walked to the row he was sitting in. Their professor gave the groups time to discuss the logistics of the project.

"Hey. I'm Azima," she introduced herself by sticking her hand out. He glanced at it, then glanced at her boobs, disinterested.

"Waddup?" he dryly responded.

Azima's cheeks flushed due to her taupe colored skin. She was on the slender side, with medium-sized breasts. Her campus attire was never anything special, but maybe after today, she would put more effort into her appearance.

Swallowing her embarrassment, she decided to press forward. She was a secretary in the psychology department, and she had to figure out a way to work around her schedule.

"So... um... yeah... we're partners. What's your schedule like? I have a job on campus, so maybe we can meet –"

"Aye. I ain't gon lie to you... I don't plan on taking this shit too serious. Hit me up whenever, though. I can work you in my schedule. You got Instagram?" he cut her off.

Azima's brows furrowed, and she blinked at him. She couldn't imagine not taking a class *too serious*, perhaps it was the overachiever in her. She always had perfect grades, perfect attendance, turned in every assignment, and even did extra credit and tutored when she didn't have to.

What exactly did this nigga think this was?

"Um... yeah... I got Instagram," she stammered. He looked at her, and she typed his name into the search bar, a profile for *LadiesMan-Harris* popping up. He had over ten thousand followers and followed zero people.

Typical.

Azima clicked the follow button anyway, then noticed that it was time for her to get to her job. Saying a quick goodbye, she scurried out of his row and went to her job, feeling disoriented. It was about to be a long few weeks.

Two Weeks Later

Azima finally managed to get Makeem to meet her for a late-night work session. Their project was due in another two weeks and was worth forty percent of their overall grade. Azima wanted to maintain her A+ average, so she figured that they should get a move on it, considering nothing had been done so far.

Makeem sauntered into the study room, donning a football jersey with his number 32 plastered proudly across his chest. Without greeting her, he sank into the chair and looked at Azima like he was bored.

Azima had had enough. She slammed her laptop shut and glared at him, seething. She wasn't one to usually curse someone out, but something had to give.

"I don't know what you think this is," she gritted lowly. "But you got me fucked up if you think that I'm gonna be the only one pulling my weight on this fuckin' project. If yo' half cripple ass don't wanna be my partner, then I'll go to Professor Harper tomorrow and request a change, or request that I present solo. But ain't no way in hell you gon do little to nothing and think you gone get a A offa me!"

Makeem's jaw dropped. No woman ever cursed him out before, let alone over a group project. He had Azima all wrong. Underneath that quiet demeanor, she had a beast lurking on the inside of her, and the thought both intrigued him and... made his dick hard.

Quickly recovering from his shock, Makeem rose to his full height and reached out to grab Azima before she stormed out. Her body stilled, and she glared at his hand on her arm, daring him to say something stupid.

"Aye. My bad... It's been a lot going on," he uttered, sounding slightly regretful.

"If by 'a lot' you mean fucking every hoe and professor on this campus, you can save the excuses," Azima spat.

And he couldn't help it, but the corners of his mouth turned up slyly. "You saw my video?" he had the nerve to ask, not in the least bit embarrassed.

Azima's cheeks flushed pink, and she scoffed, shaking herself from his light grip and walked towards the door. She was extremely irritated and also extremely turned on, so she needed to get away from him ASAP.

"Aye! Look, man... I'm sorry. If I don't pass this class, I won't be able to graduate. I'm already on thin ice. Just... tell me what I gotta do to get back in yo good graces." His eyes shone with sincerity, and weakly, Azima melted.

She took a deep breath and slowly walked to the table, taking a seat across from him. Inwardly, Makeem grinned, his charm working as he expected it to. Azima intrigued him, and he planned to get her right where he wanted, right on his dick.

It was from that group project that a rapport began to build between them, and Azima reasoned that beneath the cocky exterior, Makeem wasn't so bad.

If only she'd taken heed to her gut feelings.

3

"Excuse me, do you know where the criminal psychology department is?"

Azima paused from typing her research paper and glanced at the honey-hued beauty before her. She had seen her a few times on campus, draped in her cheerleading uniform, dancing at homecoming pep rallies, and even saw that she won Homecoming Queen one year.

"This is the Criminal Psych Department. Do you have a meeting with someone?" she asked, pulling up a few of the calendars to see where she should direct her. Xaharia told her that she was actually trying to see if she could sign up for tutoring, since she was failing her required class and needed it to graduate next year.

"Well... it seems you're in the right place, because I tutor as well," Azima offered. From there, the ladies exchanged phone numbers and agreed to meet later that evening in Howard Library.

Once evening came, Azima and Xaharia made small talk, and it dawned on Azima that this was one of the first times she felt like she was actually making a friend. Throughout the years, she'd always been introverted and stayed to herself. It became even worse when her mother died, and she moved off campus. Aside from the few people she interacted with in the Psych Department and now Makeem, Azima didn't have any friends.

Until Xaharia. They took a liking to each other, hanging out on campus, and Xaharia even convinced Azima to go to a few athlete and fraternity parties with her. It was outside of her comfort zone, but for the most part, Azima enjoyed herself.

"WHEW, girl! That nigga is *so fine*!" Xaharia began fanning herself, causing Azima to burst into laughter. They were in the student center cafe, having lunch together before their classes started. Makeem was the person she was referring to, and Azima's stomach fluttered. He walked past, flashing them both a sly grin, and Xaharia almost purred as her eyes followed him. Shaking her head, she took a sip of her chocolate shake and sighed wistfully.

"Nigga's just too fine for his own good. I should go give him my number, shouldn't I?" she wondered aloud. Azima's stomach fluttered again.

No.

No, you shouldn't, Azima thought to herself.

Makeem came over to their table, turned a chair backwards, and gave both ladies an impish grin.

"Ladies," he said, looking right at Xaharia, who was licking her glossed lips and twirling a curl around her finger. He then turned his salacious gaze to Azima and leaned in, giving her a peck on the lips.

Azima blanched, and it felt as if all the chatter in the Student Center went still. All eyes were on them, and murmurs of Makeem Harris publicly staking claim on a random girl began to travel like wildfire. Without another word, Makeem stood up and walked towards his crowd of friends who clowned him.

Carefully, Azima turned her head to stare at Xaharia, who had her glossed lips pressed together, staring back at her.

"That's you?" she asked in bewilderment. In Xaharia's mind, Azima was a cute girl, but not cute enough to pull a man of Makeem's caliber. Xaharia just knew that in a few days, he would be scratching the itch she had developed for him, and then go ahead about her business, like she usually did when it came to guys on campus.

Azima had thrown a wrench in her plans.

Sheepishly, Azima nodded, tucking a piece of her hair behind her ear.

"Something like that."

Her and Makeem just happened. It's like after she snapped on him for not pulling his weight for their group project, he started paying attention to her more.

Started showing up on time.

Started flirting with her more.

And when he leaned in to kiss her after walking her to her car, Azima folded like a bag of laundry.

By that evening, he was in her bed, touching parts of her that hadn't been touched in years.

Now, he was somewhat staking a claim on her publicly, and Azima didn't quite know what to make of it.

Xaharia nodded.

Once.

Twice.

Three times, another question on the tip of her tongue. Azima observed her and could almost guess the thoughts swirling around in her head.

"My bad then, sis. You better claim your man then!" Xaharia winked and continued to sip on her shake. Deep down, Xaharia was feeling salty, and she wondered what Azima had that she didn't.

Azima had a weird feeling but ignored it. It wouldn't be until a few years later that she wished she didn't.

4

SIX YEARS LATER

"Baby, how do you feel about threesomes? Would you ever want to have one?" Makeem asked over breakfast one morning, and Azima almost dropped her coffee. Tilting her head, she observed the man that she'd grown to fall deeply in love with over the years. They'd graduated and started a life together. Azima graduated summa cum laude and started graduate school studying forensic psychology, and aimed to get employed at a prison or mental hospital once she was done. When she graduated, she'd done exactly that and was a lead forensic psychologist at the state hospital. Xaharia took a different route and got employed as a corrections officer at the local women's prison. She and Azima developed a close friendship, even considering each other best friends.

And Makeem.... Well, his NFL dreams never quite panned out how he wanted, after only one year of playing pro before he suffered yet another injury to his Achilles tendon. Family connections had him as a coach, but he ended up getting cut after only two seasons. These days, he half-way pushed papers around at one of his father's offices, still unsure of what he wanted to do with his life. Azima was the breadwinner in their household, and some days, he resented it.

She often came home tired or too stressed out to have sex with him, something Makeem wasn't used to.

"Where... where did that question come from, Makeem?" Azima replied evenly, looking at him over the bridge of her nose.

"I'm just saying, baby! You with another bitch–I mean woman–would be sexy," he gave her one of his infamous lustful grins, damn near closing his eyes and groaning at the thought.

Azima's heart started racing. Just last month, she was crying to Xaharia about Makeem's distance in their relationship. Xaharia had mentioned something similar, and Azima's stance was still the same. She respected people who were fluid in their sexuality, but she was pretty sure that she was one hundred percent straight, *and* she wasn't interested in sharing her man. Makeem Harris was *hers*, and she had the mental and emotional battle scars to prove it. Dealing with a man like Makeem was a lot, on top of a demanding job where she worked for the state hospital, assessing and treating those who committed heinous crimes due to their mental state. It was no secret that Makeem enjoyed attention from the ladies. While she didn't have concrete proof that he cheated on her, her gut was telling her something. Azima also realized that she was turning into her worst fear:

Her mother.

The one who bore it all, grinned through it, and turned the other cheek towards her father's infidelity.

"Makeem... don't play with me," she remarked with more bite in her tone than she intended, but she didn't care. Indignantly, his eyes rolled, and in lieu of response, he sipped on his orange juice.

"Loosen up, bae."

They held each other's gazes for a moment, and Azima decided to take the high road. She had approximately ten minutes before she had to leave out for work, and she wasn't in the mood to get caught in Chicago's traffic. Finishing up breakfast in silence, Makeem hastily kissed her cheek and rushed to finish getting dressed himself, since he said his father was calling an important meeting today. Azima headed to her car and made the forty-five-minute drive in silence for twenty minutes before she hit her phone to call Xaharia. She picked up on the third ring as always.

"I thought you would be at work today until I checked your location," Azima said after greeting her.

"I'm uhhhh...sick," Xaharia coughed.

"Do you want me to swing by and bring you anything when I get off?"

Xaharia shook her head as if she could be seen. "No... Imma have my boo bring stuff," she snickered. For the past year, Xaharia had a secret boo that Azima had yet to meet, but it was mostly due to the fact that he lived out of town. Xaharia often traveled out of town so she could see him.

"Ohhh your boo? Well, I hope you'll stop hiding him and let me meet him soon. We could double date!" Azima said excitedly, merging into traffic.

Xaharia laughed coyly. "Girl, Makeem is not the type of nigga who would wanna go on a double date!"

A gnawing feeling settled into Azima's bones, and she remembered why she had called her in the first place. "So... speaking of, he asked me a weird ass question this morning, and I don't know what to make of it. He asked how I felt about threesomes... said that me and another woman would be sexy."

"I mean... It's just a question, Zima. Shit, how *do* you feel about it?" Xaharia coolly checked her temperature. Azima sighed, tired of repeating herself about the same thing, to the two people she cared about the most.

"I told him not to play with me. Like I told you, I'm not here to yuck anybody's yum, but certain things just aren't for me. But now I'm thinking...maybe his question is an underlying desire or need of his that he feels is unmet." Azima's therapist brain was now on as she switched lanes and zoomed carefully down the expressway.

Xaharia sighed deeply, feeling like she wasn't high enough to calm Azima down. Over the years, she'd learned what exactly made the usually impassive woman tick. Most of it surrounded the death of her mother, her father's betrayal and abandonment when her mother wasn't even cold in the ground, and Makeem. In Xaharia's opinion, she didn't understand what kept Makeem and Azima together, but she would never express that to her best friend. Everyone knew that Makeem was the biggest hoe in college and that he had an insatiable sexual appetite. It surprised everyone when he settled down with Azima.

"Look, this my other line friend. I forgot to tell my boss that I was calling in today. Check on me later?" she smoothly lied, looking at the man who claimed her pussy and slowly her heart for the past year, enter her doorway. The line went silent, and Xaharia looked to make sure that Azima hadn't hung up on her.

" 'Zima?"

"My bad, my brain is elsewhere. Yeah, I'll check on you later, and I hope you feel better," she said and then ended the call. Pulling into her designated spot, she tried to ignore the gnawing feeling in her stomach and focus on the workday.

"Now, where were we?" Xaharia smirked and crawled to the fine specimen before her, already wet with anticipation. He returned his own impish grin as her hands went to the waistband of his boxers, where she removed his hard member. His hands went immediately into the messy updo he paid for a few days ago when he felt himself hit the back of her throat. He groaned out, thanking God for the throat goat that was Xaharia Evans.

Makeem!" Xaharia frowned and popped him out of her mouth.

"Don't fuck my hair up nigga!"

"Shit.... I'll just pay for it again," he replied, feeling his dick hit the back of her throat as she drained him of everything

AZIMA SURPRISINGLY HAD a light case load for today and decided to exercise her free will and leave work early. Over the years, the overachiever in her relaxed, barely. She worked a lot, but she wanted to be the best of the best when it came to forensic psychology. The *Law & Order: SVU* episodes and true crime documentaries she binged didn't have shit on what she saw and heard while working at the state hospital.

Her stomach grumbled, so after stopping by Ain't She Sweet for her usual jerk salmon wrap, she called to see if Xaharia was feeling better and needed anything. She didn't answer, so she checked her location, and surprisingly, it was off. Looking at the time, she noticed that a few times out of the week, around 2 PM, her location would be off. She knew reception in the prison was spotty, but today Xaharia took off.

So why was her location off? That icky feeling came up again and sent a chill through her body, even though her air was already on for the warm summer day.

"Maybe I'll just check on her and drop her off some Vicks or something," Azima reasoned aloud to herself as she took the streets to Azima's bungalow. She parked right in the driveway and sent her a quick text.

> I called earlier. I stopped by the store and grabbed you some Vicks. Imma leave it on your table then head home.

Azima walked on tired legs and let herself in using the code to Xaharia's keypad that she had access to.

SLAP!

SLAP!

SLAP!

"Mmmmm. Yes! Right there! Right there! Right fucking there, Mak–"

Everything in Azima's hands fell as her eyes popped out of her head. With an open concept kitchen and living room, Xaharia was bent over the kitchen counter while Makeem plowed into her feverishly. She watched them for what felt like hours, and when Xaharia finally looked up and locked eyes with her, her trance was broken.

"AZIMA! WHAT THE FUCK– MAKEEM! MAKEEM! STOP!" she yelled, and Makeem finally stopped and looked up, not an ounce of guilt in his eyes. Azima's voice was mute, and she felt like she had lost her ability to hear as well. She gulped and leaned on the wall for balance.

"Zi–"

But Azima shook her head, refusing to see what was in front of her face or let her offer some type of excuse.

Not Xaharia was fucking her man in her own home while her man should've been at an important meeting that his father called.

Not Makeem cheating. Though it wasn't super surprising. She'd always had a hunch, but she never had concrete proof.

Until now.

Now, she had butt-naked, nasty-ass, betrayal truth.

Makeem said nothing, just dislodged himself, and she noticed his pole was glistening unprotected with Xaharia's juices. The two women stared at each other as he walked around them, disappearing into Xaharia's bedroom. Moments later, he reappeared fully dressed, car keys in hand.

"Imma let y'all work this out," arrogance dripped from his tone, and with that, he slammed the door on his way out.

"Azima, this is your fault!" Xaharia hollered, and Azima tilted her head back and chuckled mirthlessly.

"Excuse me?"

"Yeah, you knew I liked him in college! Then y'all go and get in a relationship. Okay, cool. But then you started working, being too tired for him and denying him of his needs... You couldn't even give the man a little threesome. So yeah, hoe. This is *your* fault. *Fuck you!*"

Azima took a deep breath. She wasn't a fighter, and she knew this because she had never been in one. She wasn't a killer either, though she had plenty of ideas on how to get rid of them both. Xaharia kept ranting and raving, blaming her poor behavior on Azima. The same Azima who was there for her in plenty of her high and low moments.

It was Azima who wrote her recommendation letter so she could get into her graduate school program, which she later dropped out of.

It was Azima who held her hand and picked her up after she had had countless abortions over the years because she refused to just get a tubal ligation since she didn't want kids.

It was Azima who even gave her the down payment money to buy this house, since she got laid off right before she was set to close on it.

It was Azima who gave advice, planned lavish birthday celebrations, and thought she had a sister in Xaharia. But now this same woman was in her face, blaming *her* for getting caught fucking *her* nigga?

Sometimes, the jokes write themselves.

"...And if you try to do anything to me hoe, I will get your license stripped from you so fast! Get the fuck out my house and don't come back! That's *OUR* nigga now!" Spittle flew from Xahria's mouth and landed lightly on Azima's nose.

Something inside her snapped. Sneering, Azima walked closer to her, and Xaharia backed up, fearing for her life. Azima was usually calm, but any other person in this situation would be wilding right now.

Why isn't she trying to beat my ass? She wondered to herself. Chills soared through her naked frame, making her nipples harden.

"By the time I get done with the both of ya'll, you gone wish you never crossed me," she said blankly.

"GET THE FUCK OUT MY HOUSE!" Xaharia repeated.

With her head held high, but her heart shattered, Azima did exactly what she asked.

AZIMA PULLED up to the home that she and Makeem shared and paused from entering her foyer. Makeem's Trackhawk was there, and she dreaded seeing him inside. What hurt her the most about the entire ordeal was the lack of remorse on his face.

How he cooly just pulled out of Xaharia, walked to her bathroom, washed his dick, and put his clothes on like nothing had happened.

"Imma let ya'll work this out" played on a callous loop in her mind. She'd always known that Makeem could be a dickhead, but she'd thought that he'd outgrown his brash ways the closer they got to pushing thirty.

But this wasn't just a lack of emotional maturity or callousness on his part.

This was pure, unadulterated cruelty.

This couldn't be overlooked.

Not with all she had done to prove herself worthy of his partnership.

How she did all his homework on top of her own during their senior year, when the school board refused to give him any more passes for his conduct and threatened not to graduate him unless he improved academically.

How she stayed by his side when his pro NFL dreams were cut after his second injury, and no amount of money or prestige would get him back on that field.

How she'd taken on the role of being the sole breadwinner because his parents refused to let him touch his trust fund until he figured out what he wanted to do with his life. Everyone in Makeem's immediate circle coddled him, Azima included.

She'd been a doctor, nurse, therapist, secretary, tutor, cheerleader, and lover for years.

And all for what?

To get betrayed by the only woman whom she considered a friend? Fuck that, a *sister*?

Her jaw clenched. Walking slowly over the threshold, the first level of their two-story home was quiet.

There wasn't a sound coming from his game room.

The lights were off in the kitchen.

The living room was silent.

That could only mean he was upstairs.

Azima made a beeline for the basement and grabbed a bottle of scotch from the built-in bar. She didn't drink much, but when she did, she preferred something dark and smooth.

"Alexa, play *Rocket Love* by Stevie Wonder," she announced to the device, and Stevie's words filled the space as she mulled over her feelings. Her mama used to pour the same brown liquid and play this record whenever her father would get reckless with his behavior. She used to crawl up in her mama's lap, wiping her tears until she got old enough to understand why she was crying.

Giving your all to someone, and they just disregard you?

Getting betrayed by someone you called sister and friend?

Tuh. You'd get blindly drunk and play Stevie Wonder songs, too.

Azima gripped her glass so tight, it broke, and the shards cutting her palm didn't even faze her. Tears rolled down her cheeks, and she didn't bother to wipe them.

Azima had turned into her mother.

But unlike her, she was gon' get her lick back.

5

ONE MONTH LATER

Things in Azima and Makeem's household were...quiet. Makeem knew that Azima had a spicy side, and he was sure that she would destroy his shit, try to whoop Xaharia's ass, or what he desperately wanted – breakup with his ass. Instead of being courageous enough to end things between them, he decided he would act distant from time to time, which only made her try harder. So, he decided to start fucking Xaharia, something that happened once already in college, but picked up again over the years. And he was enjoying it, until they got caught.

He rolled out of bed after having a disturbing dream. He dreamed that one moment, he was outside, kicking shit with some of his old football homies, and the next moment, three niggas bigger than him circled him and injected him with something that made him pass out before he could run. When he came to, he was in a cold and dingy basement, sitting upright in a metal chair where his hands and feet were bound with thick rope and zip ties. Heels clacking against the concrete made him wake up out of his groggy state, and he came face to face with Azima dressed in all black.

Then he woke up.

Shaking off an eerie feeling, Makeem ambled to the bathroom

and handled his morning business. The smell of eggs and bacon wafted through the air and tickled his stomach. Usually, he would be trying to text Xaharia to take off work and come ride his dick, but she'd been a little standoffish since they got caught. He couldn't believe that the girl had a conscious after this whole thing was her idea anyway. Yeah, he always thought she was attractive, but he wouldn't fuck her unless Azima blessed him with a threesome. After turning him down, Makeem felt even more justified in his decisions that happened way before he asked Azima how she felt about it. Walking down to the kitchen, Azima had his food plated, but she was nowhere to be found. Since the incident, she didn't have much conversation for him, and that was strange to him. Azima was naturally a woman of few words, but over the years, she'd open up to him. Mostly about work but also about her feelings, her fears, and her dreams, which Makeem paid halfway attention to. Following the sound of the TV blaring downstairs to the basement, he found Azima curled up in one of the recliner chairs, watching *Kill Bill* and sipping a glass of scotch with exactly one ice cube in it.

"No work today?" he announced himself, and she looked back at him with four pairs of sad eyes. A pang of guilt washed over him, but disappeared as quickly as it appeared. In Makeem's mind, no one was forcing Azima to be with him, and a woman who actually cared about herself would leave him. Azima was very smart, damn near a genius, really, but seemed very green when it came to relationships. Makeem had always done whatever it was that he wanted when it came to women, and they all overlooked it. He didn't mean to settle down with Azima, and while he couldn't say that he was in love with her, he did recognize that he didn't want her *not* to be a part of his life. He liked having access to Azima and what she offered him.

Any other woman would've left him high and dry since he got cut twice from the NFL as both a player and a coach. Not Azima, though; she loved him no matter what.

"I'm taking some time off," she softly replied and turned back to the projector screen.

Makeem's brows kissed. "The fuck you doing that for?"

Azima ignored his question and stood, making her way to the bar. Makeem's eyes swept over her frame and noticed that she had started looking thinner than usual in her lavender colored lounge dress. Over the years, her shape evolved into what one would call slim thick, but now it seemed as if her ass was losing its plumpness.

"You want an Old Fashion?" She held up the bottle of brown liquor as she started sorting the ingredients. Makeem nodded and walked to the other recliner chair, snatching the remote to find something else to watch. Moments later, she walked over with both their drinks, placing them on the tray between them. Makeem sipped his slowly, noting that it had an extra sweetness to it that he liked. One thing about it, Azima could make a good drink. Moments of silence passed between them, and after a while, Makeem felt drowsy.

Once she made sure he was good and asleep, Azima went to his side of the chair and picked up his phone. Holding up his phone for face recognition, it unlocked, and she went right to his banking app and kissed her teeth.

Nigga only had seventy-five thousand dollars in his account. His father's company paid him handsomely, even though he was nothing more than a lowly secretary who was too busy fucking her best friend to show up for work every day. Once she confirmed the transaction, all of his money went into her account, since she'd linked them.

Azima scoffed to herself. Nigga never offered one red cent on the mortgage but had seventy-five thousand casually sitting in his account. Her eyes went to slits as she went over to his text messages. At the very top was Xaharia's contact, with seven unread messages sitting there.

Don't you look bitch, she willed to herself. But temptation was too potent, and when she opened her messages, she wished she had listened to her first mind. Seven different photos of her pussy sent in invisible ink with the message *"I miss you Zaddy"* made Makeem's phone feel like hot coal in her hand. Quietly, she replaced the device back in its spot, then knocked over his glass, startling him.

"Sorry," she offered to get the broom and start cleaning up.

Makeem looked confused. "How...how long I been out?"

Azima shrugged. “I don’t know, maybe like twenty, thirty minutes. I dozed off, too,” she lied. Makeem grunted, then checked the time on his phone.

“My eyes blurry then a muthafucka. But aye, I got a move to make,” he said. Getting up to stretch, he looked at Azima and sighed. “Enjoy yo off day.”

He took slow steps to the stairs, wondering why he felt so tired all of a sudden. Getting into his car, he shot a text to Xaharia and told her that he was pulling up in less than ten minutes.

But as soon as he made a left to turn onto her street, a tree he had never seen before popped out at him, forcing him to slam on his brakes and brace himself for impact.

BOOM!

Makeem crashed, or maybe it was the tree that crashed into him, and everything went black.

“Ms. McKnight? This is Dr. Emory Roseland, calling from St. Holly Hospital. I’m calling in connection to a… Makeem Harris,” a woman’s voice announced once Azima picked up on the third ring.

The corners of Azima’s mouth turned up. The methanol she put in Makeem’s drink had the exact effect that she knew it would have on him. She also knew that once he saw Xaharia’s text, his thirsty ass would be on his way, despite being in no position to drive.

“Y-y-yes. This is she. What’s wrong with Makeem?” she laid it on thick, sounding more distraught than she actually was. She didn’t want to kill him. But she definitely wanted to make him *feel it,* for what he did to her.

“I can’t give much detail over the phone, but you need to get here as soon as you can. There’s been a terrible accident, and some questionable substances have been found in his blood. See you soon?”

Azima confirmed that she would be there as soon as possible and took her sweet time getting there. After entering the building, her act of a concerned girlfriend came back into play. A nurse escorted her to his room, where his parents, Xaharia, and two detectives were present. Azima's relationship with his parents was cordial. She always felt like they didn't like her very much, and for once, Azima didn't care enough to try and get those people to like her. It was bad enough that she did it for so many years with their son.

"Hi, Mr. and Mrs. Harris," she greeted. She and Xaharia locked eyes, and Azima's fists balled. She would give anything to put her in a hospital bed right next to Makeem, but she had plans for her, too.

The shorter detective cleared his throat. "Now that everyone's here, I wanted to say that this accident calls for some investigation. Medical personnel informed us that there were obscene levels of methanol in his bloodstream, enough to kill a horse. We believe the poison obscured his vision while driving, causing him to hallucinate and ram into a light pole at the end of Indiana Street. You all are the closest to him. Tell me, would there be anyone you could think of that may have a vendetta against your son?"

Makeem's parents exchanged puzzled glances while Xaharia and Azima locked eyes again, and Azima smiled smugly. All the color drained from Xaharia's face, while it clicked. Makeem was on the way to her house. Before that, a random phone number texted her, with the simple words, "*Your time is running out.*"

Xaharia didn't think anything of it, at first. She figured it was the wrong number or just someone playing on her phone. But now....

Nah. This hoe ain't that crazy, she thought to herself. *Or is she?*

Xaharia mentally checked out, trying to think of a way that she could get out of this hospital. The only reason she was here was because when she called him, the paramedics answered his phone, and she quickly threw on clothes and rushed over here. She didn't love Makeem, but they did have a bond that was enough for her to betray the girl who considered her a sister and a best friend.

All eyes turned to Azima, and she clutched her chest. "Methanol?

What in the world is that? Makeem doesn't have any enemies, does he?" She glanced at his distraught parents. Then she glanced at Xaharia and gave her a meek smile. "Thank you so much for being here, bestie. How did you know what happened?"

Xaharia swallowed, feeling as if she was backed into a corner. Azima was playing dirty, and she didn't like it one bit.

"I.... I called looking for you. After you didn't answer. Called to make sure we were still on for lunch later today. And... the paramedics answered and said what happened," she replied faintly. Azima's eyes began to water, and she glanced at a sleeping Makeem. The tubes all in his nose made his chest rise and fall unnaturally, but she knew he wasn't dead.

Only close to it.

"Thank God for you. The doctor called me shortly after." She crossed over to Xaharia and leaned in for a hug. Leaning close, she whispered so only she could hear.

"Your time is running out, Xaharia. I hope it was worth it."

"WHY IS seventy-five thousand dollars from my son's account missing, Azima?" It was the first question that Mr. Harris asked her once she answered on the third ring. Makeem had just gotten released from the hospital a couple of days ago, and instead of coming back to the home he shared with Azima, his parents felt it would be best if he stayed under their watchful eye. That was fine with Azima. It gave her more time to think about her next move. The methanol ended up not penetrating his system too deeply since he only had one drink. He was able to start Hemodialysis immediately, which prevented death, but his vision was still touch-and-go.

"Mr. Harris... I– I'm not sure what you're talking about," she replied. She was sitting at the kitchen counter, sipping on a glass of red wine while typing in her client notes.

"Bullshit, Azima! You know, I've never really cared for you... Makeem could certainly do better, but the boy is grown, so I allowed it. Then he gets into this accident, and all of a sudden, seventy-five thousand from his account is missing and somehow in yours! Are you stealing from my son, Azima?"

Azima grinned. Mr. Harris admitting to disliking her didn't shock her one bit. The few times she was around Makeem's parents, they were cordial but standoffish, especially him. Maybe they envisioned their son being with someone completely different from her, someone who matched their haughty and over-inflated lifestyle, even though their son was a fucking failure.

"You know what, Mr. Harris, it's okay that you don't care for me because the feeling is very much mutual. Calling my phone as if I don't pay every bill in this fucking house, while your incompetent son barely pushes papers around at your failing oil company, is comical at best. And to accuse me of stealing is –"

"The proof is right in front of me, bitch! That's alright, the authorities are on the way to your door as we speak. Seems like you need to be put under investigation too, you thieving ass bitch!"

Azima hung up on him and smiled. The adrenaline rush she got from carrying out various parts of her plan invigorated her. In a way, she felt like she wasn't only getting her vengeance but also the vengeance that her mother couldn't get. Azima's father constantly played in her mother's face, and it possibly killed her more than the cervical cancer did.

You don't think you're taking things too far? She asked herself.

"Hell nah," she answered herself audibly.

DING-DONG!

DING-DONG!

DING-DONG!

Azima drained the last of her wine in her glass and walked to the sink to rinse it out and drop it in the dishwasher. She then checked over her appearance in the hallway mirror and noted how well put together she looked in the grey two piece Hustle Honeyz sweatsuit. Her bob was freshly cut and styled, and though sans makeup, her skin looked fresh and supple.

She swung the door open. "Good afternoon, officers. How may I help you?"

"Miss McKnight. We're here on behalf of the Harris family. They've listed you as a possible suspect for the poisoning of a Makeem Harris." How it escalated from stealing from him to poisoning him was no surprise. Smart people looked to everyone closest to a victim first. That's why when her heart rate accelerated, she got quiet.

She didn't cry.

She didn't scream.

She didn't protest.

She didn't confirm or deny.

She simply closed her door behind her and held her wrists out.

"Okay." Her voice and facial expression were void of emotion.

The officers glanced at each other and then read her her Miranda Rights and placed her in the squad car, without realizing that the next phase of her plan was in motion.

6

"Miss Azima McKnight. Twenty-eight years old. Forensic Psychologist at the state's hospital. Girlfriend of Makeem Harris for the past six years. College-sweet-hearts. Can you tell me how seventy-five thousand dollars of his money ended up in your account about two weeks ago?" An olive-skinned detective with dark hair slid a bank statement across the table towards her. Azima held his eye contact and merely glanced at the slip of paper.

"I moved it."

"Why? Mr. Harris comes from a powerful family. He suffered a near-fatal car accident as well. Did someone pressure you to do that?"

"No. No one pressured me."

"So why–"

Azima leaned up on the metal table, her eyes bouncing around the grey walls and ugly fluorescent lights, and landing back on the olive-skinned detective. A steaming cup of coffee that she'd let go cold was on her right. Azima was bored and wanted to get this over with, but she knew that after her confession, she'd have to start the process of awaiting trial.

"Have you ever cheated on your wife, Detective...," she glanced at his badge, "Detective Schapelli? Have you ever fucked a woman that she considered a sister or friend? Have you ever betrayed your wife or girlfriend like that?"

Detective Schapelli's brows kissed. "I'm not sure why that has to do with –"

"Just answer the question," she commanded softly. "I won't judge you."

Silence lingered in the air, and Azima accepted his lack of loquacity as an omission of the truth he wanted to avoid.

Detective Schapelli shifted in his seat uncomfortably and cleared his throat. "Miss McKnight, the day of Mr. Harris' accident, there was an unusual substance found in his bloodstream. Methanol, and not the kind that's usually found in alcohol. A stronger, more potent version that is harmful if consumed by mouth. Did he consume anything before he left?"

Azima's lips curled. "Yes, he had a glass of scotch."

"And at what time was this?"

Azima shrugged. "Maybe eleven, or twelve o'clock. He came to watch a movie with me, and I offered to make him a drink."

Detective Schapelli shifted uncomfortably in his seat. Was this girl admitting she tried to poison this man? He was almost afraid to ask her the next question.

"Miss McKnight, I understand that you are a forensic psychologist. How is your personal mental state?"

Azima shrugged. "It could be better, considering all things. After finding out he cheated on me with a woman I considered my sister and best friend, something inside me snapped."

"What do you mean by that?"

Azima smiled wickedly and leaned up on the table and brought her voice down to a whisper again.

"I mean... that I'm the one who poisoned him."

Azima's confession did exactly what she needed it to do. The detectives called in some forensic psychiatrists to evaluate her mental state for temporary insanity. They didn't believe that a woman who presented herself in the way that she did was capable of committing such a crime.

She was a good employee, a straight-A student all her life, and a pillar in the community. Azima refused private legal counsel, opting for a public defender who was so meek, she wondered how he'd fare outside of law school. The legal system was a shark-eat-shark world, and this white boy was looking like fish food. After her evaluation determined that she wasn't temporarily insane, she was then ordered to go to trial. The judge read her sentencing, and she got ten years in total. Five for attempted murder and five for stealing the money out of his account and sending it to hers.

Azima saw the smug looks on Mr. and Mrs. Harris' faces after the verdict was read and she was remanded. Before that, Mr. and Mrs. Harris were each able to give a victim impact statement because Makeem was still suffering from ocular impairment and limited use of his voice.

"Ms. McKnight and our son started dating in college, but I knew she was never the right fit for him. She was intelligent, but I always had a feeling that she was up to no good. We would like to thank the courts for punishing her to the full extent of the law," their lawyer read in a joint statement.

Azima's character was attacked at every angle, and she knew she looked crazy. But she still had one more thing to do.

After closing statements from her public defender and getting handcuffed, the rest of the day was a blur as she got ready for transport to the women's prison. She arrived, and she smiled maniacally. Right at the entryway, Xaharia's face blanched. She was ordered to do the inmate intake, and the last person she thought she'd see was Azima.

Shouldn't she have been in maximum security?

"Hi, Xaharia," Azima spoke lowly. "I told you that your time was up."

The End

If I Can't Have You

PART IV

IF I CAN'T HAVE YOU

1

"You can't just spend your whole life on this block, Mamas. You gotta go away. Get out. Make sumn of yoself cuz you got the potential," said Sunni's boyfriend Sire of the last five years.

The words pierced into Sunni's heart like sharp bullets. At nineteen years old, she was one year post-grad from high school and spent her days trying to be Sire Young's wifey. She'd been in love with him since she was fourteen years old, and though her family hated him, she loved Sire with every inch of her and hated being apart from him. He was more than her man. He was her friend, confidant, partner, and safe space. She came to Sire for everything, and she wanted for nothing.

But when Sire found out that he would potentially have to do five to ten years around the same time she found out she got accepted into Southern Illinois University, he knew their fairytale romance would have to come to an end. He was a stand-up dude like that. He put everyone before him and considered everyone else's feelings before his own. It was what Sunni loved and resented about him.

Sunni fell deeply silent, a rarity for a woman who always had something to say. She was afraid that if she even uttered a syllable, she would just burst into tears, and even though Sire was her most trusted confidant, she hated crying in front of him because of how personal he took it, even when he never said or did anything wrong. He was a fixer, and from a young age, he committed himself to fixing all of Sunni's problems. But how does the cause of an issue become the balm that soothes her at the same time?

Instead, Sunni let the silence linger between them a bit more and stared out the passenger seat window. The block she grew up on, the one she met Sire on, the one she got into many fights on, the one that hosted plenty of block parties, would soon be left behind and replaced with a foreign college town six hours away.

Her chest heaved up and down.

Up and down again.

Ragged breaths threatening to seep through.

Feeling the momentum build between them, a singular tear escaped her eyelid and blurred her sight. Instinctively, Sire reached over and wiped the tear from her eye, as he had done many times before. Sunni was his heart, and he hated seeing her so overcome with emotion that *he* caused. In their five years of being together, literally growing up together, they really did love and support and shoulder a lot of burdens for one another.

They also had *never* been apart.

It was like one day they met, and then as quick as one could blink, they were glued at the hip of one another.

At twenty, the street life and constant cycle of loss hardened Sire and matured him beyond his years. He wanted more for Sunni. Not only was she drop-dead gorgeous with velvety soft, light caramel candy colored skin and dimples, and a smile that would light up the whole room, she was also insanely smart with a love for all things math and numbers.

A genius, she was. She was undecided in what she wanted to be when she grew up, but she knew that it had to involve numbers.

Maybe she'd be a renowned mathematics professor.

Maybe she'd come back to her hood and teach elementary school math and run a math camp at the same school she matriculated from.

Maybe she'd go corporate and be something fancy like a chief financial officer of a Fortune 500 company.

To Sire, the sky wasn't even the limit for Sunni. He just needed *her* to see that. Needed *her* to know that even though he loved her and needed her more than he needed air to breathe, there was *more* to life than each other.

But how could he say any of that without seeming like an asshole? Without being the bad guy? It's not like she was trying to hear him anyway.

Sire ran his hand through his shoulder-length locks, in dire need of a retwist badly. Sunni usually did that for him, but things had been so tense lately, he didn't feel comfortable lying between her legs like he used to. His retwist appointments with her, much like everything else with Sunni, were sacred.

And, if he was to convince her that she was better off without him because his circumstances would do nothing but hold her back or pause her life unnecessarily, then how would he succeed when they were still stuck in routine and going through the motions?

"Sun," he rasped. "Baby. You can't cry about it, shorty. You have to go and make something of yourself. You deserve more than to wait on me to serve my time and get out."

Sunni's silent tears led to full-on sobs, her shoulders shaking and all. While she understood that Sire was right, she was having a hard time imagining life without him, and that was the thing that hurt the most.

Co-dependent?

Maybe.

But not many understood that when you didn't have much of anything, finding a love as rare as hers and Sire's was something that didn't happen too often. They were the hood's golden couple. She, the pretty smart girl who could run numbers better than the most experienced hustler, and Sire, the dope boy with bigger dreams. Very intelligent, but the cycle of being born in the hood sidetracked him.

And though only twenty, Sire protected, honored, respected, and loved Sunni like no other.

How could she do life without him?

"It's just not fair!" The tears were coming in droves now, and her face was turning red. It was no use in trying to steel her emotions because with Sire, she could never hide too much.

Sire had done the one thing he promised never to do – and that was break her heart. He would rather go back in time and not be born than break Sunni's heart.

Sire remained silent, listening closely to her breathing. When Sunni cried, she did it with her whole body, and it always took a minute for her to stabilize.

"I'm okay now," she announced, wiping her face with the napkins she kept in Sire's glove compartment. She turned to face him, and her heart shattered again at seeing the sorrow in his eyes. Sunni took a deep breath and reached out to rub her thumb over the tattoo of her name above his left eyebrow. It was fading, because he'd gotten it done in a dilapidated house when Sunni was sixteen. Sire's jaw locked, and the only sound in the car was their breathing and the weight of their hearts breaking.

"What did you always tell me, Sy? That no matter what, we'd be together. No matter if it was hell or jail separating us. I can.... Imma still go to school. Imma become everything we talked about me being. I'll write you. Maybe I can even come visit you? And, no matter what... I will *always* love you. You are more than your mistakes. You are more than your choices. And just like you helped me believe that my dreams are limitless, yours are too." Sunni's tone changed from hesitant to speaking with conviction.

Inwardly, Sire weakly smiled.

This was it.

This was his moment.

And it would *hurt*, but it would be necessary.

He knew Sunni better than she knew herself sometimes. He knew she wasn't strong enough to withstand this yet. If at all.

He turned to face her, grabbing her hand and kissing it. Sunni's skin was always soft and smelled of cocoa butter. He relished in her softness because after today, it would be so long until he felt her again.

"Sunnita Parnell-Young," he started, calling her by her full name and tagging his last name onto it. "I loved you ever since I bumped into you while you were racing Can't Get Right down 71st street. It was crazy, cus as young as we was, I ain't never felt like that about nobody before. I fell hard and fast... but you never left me hanging."

"Baby, I-"

"Hold on. Let me finish," he continued. Sire's eyes were starting to water, and it was shattering Sunni's heart. "You a good girl... a good ass woman to me. I wouldn't be able to live with myself if I allowed you to worry about me while I'm behind that wall. I did the crime, so I gotta do the time. It's life," he shrugged. "But... you still have *more* life. You can't write me, mamas, you'll get distracted. You damn sure can't come visit me. You can still love me just as I'll always love you... But I need you to be selfish for once and love yourself a bit more."

Sunni recoiled, stunned. It was so quiet in Sire's Monte Carlo, you could hear the blades of grass blowing in the evening breeze.

"S-s-s-ire..." she stuttered. "What exactly are you saying?"

This was the part that Sire dreaded. The part that would be the nail in the coffin for Sunni, for them as a whole. This would break her, and for once, Sire couldn't put Sunni back together. His heart ached, worried about what type of person Sunni would turn into after this. Would she turn cold? Would the light she brought to every space be dimmed now?

"Sire?" Sunni's pleading voice cut through the noise in his head.

Sire licked his dry lips and felt his eyes swell with tears again.

He took a deep breath and blew out some air. "It's no easy way to say this, Sunni, but.... We have to come to an end. I can't be with you from behind the wall. I can't hold you back in life. Your future is very bright. Me? I'm just a street nigga, nothing special. But you? You are more than special. I-I-I'm sorry, baby," his voice cracked on the last part. He then squeezed his eyes shut because he couldn't face her.

Sire could face knocking a nigga off.

He could face watching a fiend give in to the vices he provided.

He could face his pending jail time with his head held high.

But he could not face the love of his life crumpling before him, all due to his decision. Contrary to how this seemed, his decision was breaking him too. He just had to be strong enough for the both of them, like he always was.

"Sire," she sighed. "Imma ask you one last time.... Emotions are high right now, baby. And, I'm trying really hard to get that, but my heart is hurting, baby... There is no me without you... If I can't have you, then what the fuck is the point of doing life? Huh?! Are you sure this is what the fuck you want?!" Sunni's voice rose two octaves while her chest heaved up and down erratically. Sire knew she was having an active panic attack, but when he reached out to grab her hand, she snatched away violently.

"DON'T FUCKIN' TOUCH ME! ANSWER ME!" She bellowed.

Sire hung his head in shame. He couldn't win for losing, but there was no true winner in this.

"I only want what's best for you, boo. And right now, I am not what's best. I love you, Sunnita, you know that," he deflected in an effort to soften the final blow. "But not being together just makes more sense... Spread your wings and fly, baby. You don't need a nigga like me holding you back."

Sunni blinked at him, her eyes blurry with tears that just would not cease coming down.

Once.

Twice.

Three times.

Then she nodded. She committed Sire's face to memory. She knew every line on his cocoa butter brown skin. Knew every coil of his locs. Could damn near count every lash on his eyes and knew every tattoo on his body.

Without another word, she turned the handle and not only exited his car, but exited his life completely.

The next morning, Sunni took the Amtrak down to Carbondale while Sire got processed into prison.

Four and a Half **Years Later**

"Excuse me, ma'am, do you know where the student center is?" A tall, burly dude with a new vending machine on a dolly stopped Sunni to ask her.

"Yeah. It's actually where I'm headed, so you can follow me," she replied, checking the time on her phone. Sunni was in the last semester of her extra senior year, and she couldn't wait to be done. She was a Finance major with a double minor in mathematics and business administration. Once she got to SIU, she transformed herself.

Started going by her full name, or allowing people to only call her "Nita."

Struggled a bit in her first semester, but then started joining different organizations to foster community and make friends.

She joined a sorority and had ten other women that she considered her sisters.

Became an RA.

Mentored other students and those in the college community.

Had her own car and apartment.

She even ran for and won homecoming queen.

Sunni – or Nita- was popular on campus, down to earth, and didn't play at all when it came to school.

But something was missing. Something that still made her heart ache, but she honored his wishes.

She didn't reach out.

She didn't send the letters she wrote.

She for damn sure didn't take that ten-hour drive and go visit him. She left him, and her life back on 71st street on a shelf where they belonged.

The burly man grunted and started pushing the dolly behind her as she zoomed across campus. Her last class of the day was in Faner Hall, and she hated that building. Damn near five years later, and she still got lost in it.

"That's the student cent–"

Time froze.

They locked eyes.

Sunni's jaw went slack, and she looked down at herself, then back up at him.

How is this even real?

"Sunni," he rasped, stepping aside the burly man and getting in her space. Sunni squared her shoulders and took a step back. Sire couldn't believe his eyes. His girl was all grown up now. This girl... well, woman was mature. Alluring. Breathtakingly beautiful. She still had skin that was the color of caramel candy that glowed differently. Her lips were fuller, face rounder, hair longer, and body thicker than he remembered. The Sunni he left was slim, but he loved her body in any way. She still smelled good, like cocoa butter and some type of floral perfume that tickled his nose and made him want to bury his face in her neck and just breathe.

"Sunnita," she corrected coldly. Sire's eyes widened. The Sunni he knew never liked being called by her full name. Who was this woman, and what did she do with the girl he left four and a half years ago?

Meanwhile, Sunni was wondering what the fuck Sire was doing here. Gone were his shoulder-length locs in dire need of a retwist. His eyes were sad, but physically, he looked good. His body was more buff. His fade reminded her of when she first met him, before he asked her to help him start his dreads because he wanted to be like Lil Durk. Her name above his eye was still intact. It even looked like he got it touched up. He was dressed in a pair of dark blue coveralls with *Forever Young Vending Co* on the back.

"Sunni," he said firmly. She squeezed her eyes shut, as if she was trying to block out a nightmare. With her voice barely above a whisper, she asked, "What are you doing here?"

Sire stepped closer, his tall body towering over hers. After all these years, Sunni's body still reacted. Her legs felt like jello. She took a deep breath, only to take in his pleasant smell of clean linen and mahogany teakwood, despite sweating in this sun all day.

Fuck.

"Sunni," he said again as if he couldn't believe that she was right here in front of him. Many nights while behind the wall, he thought of her. He dreamed of her. He wished and prayed for an opportunity to show her that he missed her and still loved her. He wanted to write her, but he didn't want to disturb her.

And cowardly, he didn't want to face how much he hurt her.

Sunni was his one true weakness. So he hardened and never spoke of her name to anyone. Good behavior got him out over a year ago, and he decided to take his former drug money and invest it in a business he and Sunni talked about owning one day. *Forever Young Vending Co.* was born, and he hired three men in addition to himself to install vending machines across college campuses and other businesses all over the United States. It took six months and a lot of trial and error to make his first legal six figures, but once he signed a multimillion-dollar deal with all of Illinois' public colleges, it enabled him to expand.

What are the odds that the expansion would make him cross paths again with the love of his life?

"I gotta go –" she turned on her heel, and gently, he grabbed her by the elbow. Sunni froze, feeling electricity shoot through her body. Sire must've felt it too because he smirked.

"Please. Let me take you somewhere tonight. The best restaurant in town. I miss you, Sunni," he pleaded.

And dammit, if the feeling wasn't mutual. It was damning how the person responsible for shattering her heart was the only person she wanted to piece it back together.

Sunni shook her head. "I can't," she whispered. Just as Sire was about to get on his knees and beg, they were interrupted.

"Nita? Babe, you're about to be late to class," Sunni's boyfriend, Avery, said. She'd been dating him for the last two years, and while she cared for him, he didn't make her feel like Sire did.

Sire's eyes turned deadly, and Sunni began to panic.

"Yeah, so the student center is just right across there. Nice meeting you," she rushed out, taking hold of Avery's hand before he got knocked out.

Sire smiled, but it didn't quite reach his eyes. "I'll see you around, *Sunni*."

Sunni didn't look back, but a part of her knew in so many words that he meant exactly what he said.

Too bad, she wasn't into giving second chances.

The End

Lust

&

Liquor

PART V

LUST & LIQUOR

1

D*oes this make me a hoe now?* I thought to myself, glancing over to the snoring stranger in my bed.

I found myself stretched.

Limbs stretched.

Pussy stretched.

Mind stretched.

Earlier, I was wrist to ankle, wrapped by a thick, black, leather Tom Ford belt.

I was restrained... and I was stretched.

It was the day after Christmas. I went out on a whim after spending the day with my older brother. The year before, I spent it with my lover watching all my favorite Christmas movies in matching Christmas pajamas. We exchanged gifts and had lots of nasty sex underneath that mistletoe and by the Christmas tree.

This year, I was single. When he broke up with me two days before Valentine's Day, I didn't anticipate what the holiday season would be like.

I got through my birthday.

I got through Easter.

Memorial Day.

Juneteenth.

Fourth of July.

Sweetest Day.

Thanksgiving.

And now.....

My first Christmas without him. And I almost canceled the entire holiday. Christmas was my favorite time of the year besides my birthday, and that nigga turning out to be not who I thought he was almost gutted me. Okay, maybe I'm lying a bit. My past lover always portrayed himself exactly as he was, and *I* was the one who overlooked all the ways we didn't align. So in many ways, him leaving me did me a favor?

The verdict is still pending on that.

Going all year without someone you're used to having by your side almost made me hate all the things I loved before.

Almost.

My therapist said I needed to find a way to take my power back. That grief was just a part of life, and just because this season shared a lot of memories, that didn't mean I had to think life was over. She reminded me that change was the only constant and that while feeling scary, change often led to beautiful new beginnings.

I wanted to fire that lady right then and there on the spot. How dare she suggest that I to do all the right things when all the wrong things were more comfortable for me?

"Alicia." The stranger called me by the fake name I gave him, and the corners of my mouth turned down. Once the lust powered by the copious amounts of liquor I drank wore off, I was often disgusted by my actions.

But not enough to stop doing it every other weekend.

This week's contestant was an older man I'd met at The Promontory. Our interaction went as most of my interactions went lately.

We locked eyes.

He smirked.

I waited patiently for him to come over, while I nursed my drink.

He sauntered over, stopping short of invading my personal space.

I felt him take in my appearance, a simple outfit of Kelly green bell-bottom pants, a white turtleneck, and white boots. My hair was freshly dyed chocolate brown with honey blonde highlights, cut into layers that framed my face. I looked good, and this potential suitor knew it too.

He said his name was Kenneth or Kamari, or something of the sort. Then he asked for my name, to which I swiftly replied, "Alicia." Whole time, my name was Nakiya, but I never gave them my real name.

Our fun would only last for tonight, anyway.

The older man was handsome, too. If I were in the business of having a sugar daddy, he'd fit the bill, at least for the physical part. The financial part was yet to be determined because women often thought a nigga had money just because he was buying them drinks at the bar. Not knowing that those niggas woke up to overdrafted accounts and had to pray that their cards didn't decline. This man looked and smelled like money, though.

Salt and peppered beard.

Tapered hair that had a few curls at the top.

Well-maintained goatee.

Full, two-toned lips.

Broad shoulders.

All thirty-two of his teeth.

He was dressed in dark slacks with a Tom Ford belt and a black turtleneck with a singular Cuban link chain and smelled like a woodsy vanilla scent.

My kitty began to purr, and I felt myself about to turn into my alter ego for the night. The one who found company at the bottom of liquor bottles and covered my grief and loneliness with one-night stands. The one who didn't allow men to know the real me, court me, or treat me how I yearned to be treated.

Right now, I was doing shit just because the liquor told me to. Just because chasing that temporary satisfaction was better than dealing with my real feelings day in and day out.

"Did you drive Miss Alicia?" the man asked, his eyes sweeping over my breasts appreciatively.

I shook my head and sipped my drink again, a sidecar made with D'USSE. I didn't drive and got around just fine using ride-share services. My mood almost soured when my mind went to how my ex used to drive me everywhere.

"Then you wouldn't be opposed to enjoying the evening with me?" Seduction laced his tone. I ran my fingers along his broad chest, down his torso, and finally, down to his hardened member that was hardly contained in his slacks.

Giving it a gentle squeeze, lust twinkled in my eyes.

This will do.

"Lead the way," I replied. With that, he took my hand in his, and we skipped the party early.

LUST WAS an interesting emotion to me. It didn't get as much PR as love, or sadness, or anger, but it was just as potent. Just as harrowing, just as invigorating.

Where you had no control over love aside from choosing it, lust was more manageable. Sure, some people let lust control them, but really, it was you *trying* to control *it.*

Love hurts you.

Lust can too.

Love can gut you.

Lust can too.

Lust is what brought me back to this luxe hotel suite on the 57th floor.

Lust was what had me riding a stranger into oblivion, knowing that I would never speak to him again come daylight.

Lust let me be as obscure and as salacious as I wanted, because the real me felt broken beyond repair.

The stranger and I finished our escapade, and I quickly showered while he snored. He surprised me last night. He may have been older, but that dick absolutely was not. He had me twisted and stretched in so many positions that I may as well have gone to try out for the Universal Soul Circus after our tryst.

In another life, I'd probably take him seriously. He seemed like the type to wine you and dine and keep you fucked and full.

But I wasn't interested in any of that.

I chuckled to myself, the frost of a winter morning in Chicago stealing my breath. I opted to take the train home and pulled my flask out, hoping the burn of the dark liquid would serve as a second winter coat and as the catalyst for my next lust-filled decision.

Confessions of A Lover Girl

PART VI

CONFESSIONS OF A LOVER GIRL

1

Dear Lover Gods,

Why would you bless me with the heart I have, with the temperament I have, with all the love I have, yet damn me to what feels like loving those who don't love me back? Patience is a virtue, this I know, but for once I want someone to stick around for the long haul and not just be another lesson learned. Have I not paid for the sins of my mother and father already? I want love that stays. Love that prays. Love that purifies my pain. Love that sees me. Love that chooses me. Love that honors and cherishes me, even when my attitude isn't the best or my energy changes from day to day. Before I leave this Earth, I want to experience and hold on to love that lasts in every lifetime. I don't want a trail of tears or memories of broken hearts to follow me in my dying days.

Lovingly Yours,
Kay Cherie Amour

I sealed my journal entry with three spritzes of my perfume and sighed. Night after night, I found myself writing to the Gods of Love to bless me in that department at least. I felt cursed, like in another life I had done something so egregious that no matter how hard I tried, I just wouldn't be loved in the ways that I wanted to be loved. I had experienced heartbreak too many times to count, but I'd be a liar if I said that I wasn't the cause of a few heartbreaks as well.

I was exhausted.

Mentally.

Physically.

Emotionally.

Spiritually.

Pensively, I stared at myself in the full-length mirror perched in the corner of my bedroom and surveyed my appearance. I was beautiful, that was for sure, but not even the most beautiful woman in the world was exempt from heartbreak and pain. My beauty didn't stop at the physical, either, though many suitors got caught up in the surface level of me. They always wanted something from me, whether it was my time, my money, my pussy, my energy...

But never my heart.

Scoffing, I picked up my phone and opened Instagram, but I don't know why I did that. A scroll down my timeline showed plenty of people showing off their highlight reels of the life I wanted to live.

She got married.

They just welcomed their second child.

They're on a baecation.

He just bought his wife a house that he had built from the ground up.

The more I scrolled, the more I found myself feeling lower and lower about myself, and I had to put a stop to that.

Needed to put a stop to that.

Being single wasn't the problem.

It was the constant yearning for something that seemed so unattainable that was a problem for me. Because how was it that every other thirty-two-year-old woman had found her forever, yet here I was nursing a broken heart at my big age?

When does the shit end?

Does it ever get better?

People say it does... but my 'better' hasn't come yet.

And the irony of it all? I had to counsel people through their relationship woes while nursing my own broken heart. I was a relationship therapist at the Chicago location for Love Rehab and often felt like I should be an inpatient client myself.

I was insecurely and anxiously attached.

I didn't grow up in the healthiest environment, so I never saw healthy relationships modeled by anyone around me.

And my track record when dealing with love was full of inconsistency, infidelity, situationships, and finally, an impromptu self-love journey that's been ongoing for the past five years.

I'd be lying if I said I wasn't tired of loving myself. I wanted to love myself *and* have someone else love me, too.

I preached to my clients about the importance of setting boundaries, managing expectations, and the like, but... it wasn't something I always practiced. And I didn't sugarcoat how exhausting it was to do all that, all the time. I was perplexed as to why my fellow humans didn't have an intrinsic desire to just treat one another right.

Like, was I really asking for too much?

No, Kay, you're not.

It's just not your time yet, love.

But when you meet your next and final suitor, you'll just know.

My self-help talk track played on a loop in my mind as I unlocked the doors of my office space. It was cozy, decorated in soft greens and nudes. I preferred fresh lavender and vanilla plug-ins and kept a fresh bouquet of roses on display. I liked natural, slightly dim lighting and had affirmations and black art pieces adorning my walls. Clients often felt relaxed, able to lay down their burdens when they sat on my couch. Dr. Love spared no expense in letting her employees deck out our offices in whatever way we saw fit.

Peering at my calendar, I checked and saw that I had three clients on the books and one rescheduled. Serving the public often felt like a thankless job, but sometimes my clients had a breakthrough. My first client of the day was a twenty-two-year-old young woman who reminded me so much of myself.

She, too, was never modeled healthy relationships from those around her.

She, too, wanted to love and be loved.

She, too, wondered why her heart was made to be so big if a void was going to be left in it.

She, too, was learning and unlearning and still had a long way to grow.

I don't think we ever stopped evolving and growing.

Not when it came to love.

Not when it came to figuring out what it was that we deserved.

Not when –

"I'm saying, though, Kay... why did God make me this way if I wasn't gonna find my happily ever after? What's the point of loving at all?" she asked, twisting the strings of her hoodie. Though I had my doctorate, I kept my rapport with my clients semi-casual and allowed them to call me by my first name.

"You ask really good questions, Anaya. And you're not uncommon or alone in your thinking," I paused for a moment, letting my words sink in. "We love because...because that's just how we're wired. Humans need love; it makes the world go round. And at twenty-two, do you think that you've met all the people who will love you? Do you think God is finished with you yet? Do you think that your possibility of finding your.... *Happily Ever After* ended when your relationship from earlier this year did?"

I didn't bombard my clients with toxic positivity because I believed that feelings were valid, though not always facts. I also believed that sometimes, maybe just maybe, everyone wouldn't find their one true love, though the adolescent in me believed we would.

People often preached that there was someone out there for everyone. Shit, if you were ethically non-monogamous, there was a possibility that you had multiple *someones* for you, a person to meet every need and desire.

Anaya stared at me pensively, mulling over my questions. After a while, she shrugged her shoulders. "I don't know, Doc. It just all seems so bleak right now," she confessed.

I related to her more than she knew.

2

My evenings after work were repetitive and mundane.

Gym.
Talk to my found family.
Make or order dinner.
Journal.
Drink a glass of wine.
Mourn my old life.
Cry myself to sleep.
Wake up and do it all over again.

As sick as I was of my loneliness, I had no true desire to change my circumstances. I was too stuck in my grief. My ex-lover betrayed me so deeply that while I wanted to love and be loved, I wondered if the walls I built up would keep the good kinds of love out.

My ex-lover.

Thinking of him didn't sting as much as it used to, but an unsettled feeling still arose when I found myself catching glimpses of his new life, which started just mere months after we separated.

Betrayal from someone who used to keep you safe pierced the core. Rattled the nervous system.

Undid your trust.

Peeled you raw.

Pushed you to your breaking point.

I didn't willingly walk away from that man. My heart and my brain dragged me away.

I cried every day for months, multiple times a day. I took paid medical leave from work because at Love Rehab, the inability to control our emotions was considered a clinical and medical issue.

I still cried, but instead of multiple times a day, my tears came at night now, where the grief covered me like a weighted blanket.

No amount of therapy, healthy coping mechanisms, and redirection exercises would turn off my brain.

Time was all I had to get through this season of my life. Rumination was my downfall.

The brain was our greatest tool and our worst enemy. The patience and grace I extended to my clients, I had a hard time returning to myself.

Because here's a secret that nobody likes to talk about: all therapists did. Because despite our schooling, degrees, practicums, and accolades.... We were just mere mortals with hearts that seemed too big for our bodies.

There's no such thing as having a big heart. There is such a thing as having a lack of boundaries.

Pesky therapist talk often popped into my head. Sometimes I failed to see the nuance in the fact that we were humans. Because the truth is, maybe our hearts *were* too big for our bodies sometimes.

Some of us loved effortlessly.

Some of us caged love like it was a bird that would escape us.

Some of us gave it away too easily.

Some of us made others work for it, like it was a job.

Sipping my wine, I opened my journal to a fresh page. My mind wouldn't quiet, so that meant it was time for me to write.

March 17, 2025

Dear Lover Gods,

I'm back again.

Still lonely.

Still grieving.

Still yearning.

Still... believing.

For a while, I'd lost my belief in love and worried that I would never use my heart again. I was worried that heartbreak would be all-consuming and turn me into someone jaded. And while... I haven't mustered up the courage to fully put myself out there again, I have figured out how to breathe again, even if it's ragged, shaky breaths that come out.

In other news... the night terrors seem to stop.

I weaned myself off my anti-depressants.

I may drink a bit too much wine but that's not something I care to address right now.

Tears do still stain my pillowcase but at least the crying doesn't debilitate me anymore.

My new normal is mundane and the recalibration of my nervous system is still in progress. I'm teaching myself that the best parts of me didn't end just because that relationship did. I'm still learning that forgiveness doesn't mean that I need to reconcile with him.

Still trusting that the best is yet to come... or at least trying to believe that.

Lovingly Yours,
Kay Cherie Amour

I signed my journal entries with my name when a call came through on my line. Looking at the number, I sighed.

If hate was just misplaced love, then what was indifference towards a person? And more importantly, how did he get my number? I changed it and disappeared off the face of the earth after I crashed out on him.

But as much scrubbing of him that I tried to do from my psyche, some memories stained you, like red wine spilled on a white rug.

I watched my phone ring out, then start up again. I decided to stop being scary, and answer it. I wasn't looking for closure... the pure nosiness in me just had to see what he wanted.

"Kay," he rasped out.

"What is it that you want, Kaji?"

Kaji meant *home* in a lesser-known language, and I used to tell him all the time that he was home for me. Used to take pride in it, especially since the real home I grew up in was destitute and broken. And while we all wanted someone who reminded us of home, what if we clung to people just because it was a familiar hell? What if it wasn't solace we found in people, but familiar chaos instead?

"Did you have to send a lawyer after me, Kay?" he demanded. I closed my eyes, feeling the familiar pang of a migraine starting. The last six months were exhausting.

"Did you have to put our private videos in your little group chat without my consent? Did you have to embarrass me for all the world to see? Did you have to be dishonest when I approached you about it? Did you have to gaslight me and blame me for your indiscretion?" My chest heaved up and down.

For my man, I was whatever freak I wanted to be.

You wanted to record us? Sure.

You wanted sexy photos from me? Absolutely.

Videos of me playing with my pu–

Well, you get the drift.

But there was a responsibility that came with holding such treasures. Ones that a real man would have kept sacred. One that a man who saw me as a full human being, with real feelings, with a real need for privacy, would revere.

Kaji didn't do that.

And maybe, the reveal of his true colors was what I needed to get away from him and the illusion of safety that was our relationship.

But man, did it wreck me.

Those videos left his stupid group chat and got posted on a burner page on Twitter. My face was in it. I was known because I posted therapist content on TikTok and Instagram. People started tagging me, calling me a "Freaky Ass Therapist." And the man I freely loved, freely shared myself with, lied to my face, gaslit me, and evaded all accountability when I approached him about it.

So, I crashed out. Therapist Kay went out the window, and Kay from 71st and Sangamon popped all the way out – the one who used to be in knock-down, drag-out fights with niggas who used to try it.

Imagine my surprise when my reaction was penalized more than the cause of my distress.

Kaji sucked his teeth. "Man, I said I was sorry."

"That doesn't mean that I have to accept your apology. That doesn't mean that I have to just ignore your very real choice to do what you did. You're only sorry because you got caught. Not because you actually feel bad."

"But a lawsuit, Kay? This ain't even you, man. I thought you valued privacy," he spat.

I tittered wryly. "Shit, I thought you valued *me*."

His response was silence, so much so that I pulled my phone from my ear to make sure that the call was still connected. Although I should have hung up, there was a small part of me that wanted to see if he would grovel for my forgiveness or see how much further of a ditch he could dig himself.

"Kay...." he started. "The damage has already been done. Enough time has passed. You got the videos scrubbed from the internet anyway. We ain't together, so why do you need to lawyer up on me? You fuckin' dragging it, bro."

My teeth gnawed on my bottom lip. I was so angry. So... hurt. Indignant even, that this was my life now.

If you had told me six months ago that Kaji and I wouldn't be somewhere blissful in love, I would have called you a liar. I loved him in a way that was all-consuming and all-encompassing. I thought that I had enough love for the both of us. Even though I knew better, I believed that love was all we needed to sustain our union.

I knew now that love being all you needed was a fallacy. A fairy-tale that was packaged to and consumed by the masses.

You needed mutual respect.

You needed alignment.

You needed shared values.

You needed to hold shared morals.

You needed to have empathy.

You needed to have care.

You needed to have consideration.

And you needed to believe that love was a choice, and that contrary to how we were socialized, you do indeed choose who you love and how you show up for them.

At some point, Kaji lost the plot, and I was forced to move around.

Couldn't no amount of counseling fix what he did. I'd never look at him the same.

And that's what hurt the most.

The nigga I found home in turned out to be just as chaotically familiar as the environment I grew up in.

I drained the rest of the wine in my glass before speaking a final time tonight. "Yes, Kaji, I did.... See you in court, my nigga." Hanging up on him, I stared blankly at the space between my wall and my window.

I couldn't cry.

I didn't want to journal.

I was going numb.

But one thing I knew was that from this day forward, no man would ever have the ability to play with me like Kaji did.

I could bet my life on it.

3

Hours turned into days, and days turned into weeks, and weeks turned into months. Court came and went, and while Kaji and his stupid friends didn't serve any jail time, he was fined and ordered to pay me twenty thousand dollars for my pain and suffering. He called me all types of bitches and told me that I never had to speak on or associate myself with him again.

I didn't care, as long as that check cleared every month.

Now, it was silent in my world again. I was still journaling, the makings of a book coming together, somewhat of an autobiography with journal prompts that people could respond to. It was also weighing heavily on me to start back creating content. Since the debacle happened, I'd scrubbed my social media, creating new pages altogether and putting everything on private. *Confessions of a Lover Girl* was my brand, and on my page I discussed common issues that came up when people tried to find love – not just romantically, but in self, in community, and platonically. Starting over used to scare me, but now I've grown accustomed to it. I moved into a new condo. I had a new car. I had a new wardrobe. I had a new phone number. I even had a new dog that I named Hershey.

It was just time for me to do what my heart truly desired. I walked from my bedroom and into my newly decorated content room. I had studio lights that photographers used, a neon sign that said *Confessions of A Lover Girl* against a rose bush flower wall, and a fancy new video camera ready to record.

"My name is Kay Cheriè Amour, and you are tuned in to Confessions of A Lover Girl... Every other week, we'll unpack the ebbs and flows of love, confess some deep, sometimes dark shit, and I'll leave you with a gem to take with you." I practiced my intro, looking straight into the camera. I planned to batch record at least three videos today, edit them, then post teasers on my Instagram and TikTok, with full episodes dropping on YouTube. It felt foreign getting back into the swing of things, but I knew that over time, I'd find comfort again. Five hours later, I had everything recorded, edited, and scheduled. With dinner in the oven and a glass of wine waiting for me, I curled up on the couch with my dog and took out my journal to decompress.

July 17th, 2025

Dear Lover Gods,

The weight of heartbreak is slowly but surely easing off my mind, my body, my heart, and my soul.

I have ruminated enough.

It's time to start turning this pain, this rage, this melancholy into something more purposeful and powerful. Kaji tried, but he didn't break me.

I bloomed instead.

I must confess that before I let myself bloom, I had to let my old self rot and die. I know that there are parts of my old self that I will never get back. Grief is non-linear, yet I am finally open to welcoming the new parts of myself that have yet to be discovered. I recorded content for the first time today after what felt like centuries. Truthfully, I am nervous about showing up online again after being violated, but I can't let my fear of being perceived shy me away from what I was put on this earth to do.

I must confess that I am saddened that Kaji turned out to be just another lesson learned, but one day I'll look back on all this and be glad I learned the lesson.

I must confess that even after everything, I still yearn to love and be loved the right way. I am learning to be more patient and surrender to the season I'm in.

Lovingly Yours,
Kay Cherie Amour

The End

Saint Valentine

PART VII

SAINT VALENTINE

1

I read somewhere once that men always had a plan when they wanted to break up with you. So even if it seemed as if it came out of nowhere, it never really did.

I felt the distance between me and Rodney on our second anniversary, which fell on Christmas. His smile didn't quite reach his eyes when he looked at me. His gifts were lackluster and didn't reflect his usual thoughtfulness. Intimacy between us was lacking due to me battling my annual seasonal depression.

Things just weren't the same.

We started arguing over the pettiest things, when prior to that, we were never a couple who really argued. Yes, we had disagreements, but they never lingered for days at a time, until recently.

"What do you and your boo have planned for your birthday?" My coworker turned friend was asking as we walked down the street to our favorite salad spot. We worked at the same ad agency; her a strategist and me a copywriter. My shoulders went up and down, a fake smile painting my lips.

"I don't know, Jas.... he said it's a surprise," I lied with ease. Jas was my homegirl and all, but I refused to divulge that me and my nigga were beefing and that I hadn't heard from him in two days, forty-nine hours, and thirty-seven minutes. I often over-shared at work about how good a man that Rodney was, slight bragging about our dates, the weekly floral arrangements I would receive, and our impromptu trips. Rodney was my college sweetheart, and the topic of marriage and kids often came up – much to my delight, but maybe to his chagrin.

Maybe just maybe, he didn't see a future with me as he implied. Maybe I was a pit stop, the character development course all niggas take before they get with who they *really* want.

"Well, whatever it is, I can't wait to hear all about it next week. I love following y'all on Instagram!" She winked and then turned to order her usual.

Rodney and I had a couple's Instagram page called *The RSVP Show,* where we went live every other week playing a conversational card game that we both were obsessed with. Over wine, light bites, and an audience of a little over ten thousand followers, we would ask each other the questions and take questions from our viewers on what it was like to be in a healthy relationship.

I wonder what them same followers would think if they knew we were at odds right now.

I sent him yet another unanswered text. My lease was ending soon, and the next step in our relationship was supposed to be moving into his place together until his lease ended, and then we would buy a house. I made decent money as a senior copywriter.... He did too, as an audio engineer to the stars and a senior producer for a sports brand.

ME

Hey, its been long enough…we need to talk babe.

I WATCHED the text bubbles pop up, then disappear, then pop up again, then disappear shortly after. I waited with bated breath to see if my phone would ring. Once I realized he was still ignoring me, I powered down my phone so I could make it through my lunch and the rest of my workday.

Do you know how hard it is to focus on anything important when your nigga is ignoring you? My body was present, but my mind was on our latest disagreement we had exactly three days ago.

Three Days Earlier

We were chilling on the couch, like we always did after work on Mondays. Rodney usually picked me up from work, greeting me with flowers, and then we either swung by a spot downtown for happy hour or went straight to the grocery store to pick up items for dinner that I would cook at his house. We'd watch our shows, eat, talk, and have intimate time with each other. Sometimes we'd get on live and entertain our followers.

This particular Monday, I was beat down from work. We had a big out-of-home and digital campaign going live in just a matter of days, and I was pulling long hours and even working weekends to make sure the client was satisfied. I was also sick as a dog, in and out of urgent care, trying to get meds for whatever bug was going around. I always got sick during the winter, and I wanted nothing more than to order some pizza, drink a homemade medicine ball, and sleep.

Rodney knew this. He saw and heard how pitiful I sounded, yet still fixed his big ass lips to ask me to make us some food. I popped one eyeball open and stared at him incredulously.

"Babe... look on Instagram or TikTok and make that salmon. You have all the seasonings, and you can just pop it in the air fryer for twelve minutes." I yawned, then snuggled more under the blanket I was lying under on his couch.

"I would, babe, but you know I don't know what I'm doing in that kitchen... that's yo domain," He replied sheepishly.

"Rodney... are you serious right now?" I was feeling miserable. Could barely move. And this nigga thought I was gone get my ass up and cook?!

"Dead ass, bae. Plus, I gotta get ready and head out to The Promontory in a bit. Figured I would eat before I leave."

I popped up like a vampire. "Rodney! You see, I'm on my fuckin' deathbed bed and you're asking me to go make some fucking salmon that you can make yourself? Is yo fingers broke or what, my nigga?"

Rodney's eyes fluttered with shock. I had a mouth on me, but me and him usually communicated better than this. I was really only mean when I was sick.

"Nah. They ain't broke, but seeing as how you like to cook for us so much, I figure you would do us a solid. My bad.... You being selfish as fuck," he muttered. He got off the couch and headed to the bathroom, and I lay there wondering what the fuck just happened.

God forbid a girl just wants to be on her deathbed in peace.

Approximately twenty minutes later, Rodney came out of the bathroom with a towel wrapped around his waist. Relationship weight was a real thing, so gone was the skinny build he had when I met him in college. He was more solid, not fat per se, but you could tell that he ate good. Hell, I'd gained forty pounds myself since getting into a relationship with him.

"Wow. So you really ain't gone cook shit?"

I popped up again. "No, Rodney! I'm not!" I spat, clearly over the conversation. Slowly, I started gathering my things so that I could return home.

"Saint. You being real dramatic right now," he watched me throw my things into my bag. We usually alternated spending nights at each other's houses with one to two days to ourselves. I was taking my ass where I paid rent because if I didn't leave, Rodney's head was gonna be air-fried next.

"And **you're** *being selfish. You clearly see that I can barely hold up my own head, let alone stand over a hot stove, and you're acting incompetent like you can't use the phone that stays glued to your hand and look up a fuckin' salmon recipe!"*

For me, it wasn't about him asking me to cook. Not really. It was his lack of care that came to me when it was clear I was temporarily incapable at the moment. His selfishness gave me the ick at times.

"Technically... you wouldn't be standing over a stove. You'd be pushing a button on the air fryer," he replied smugly.

Swear to God, I almost hurled my duffel bag at him.

"STOP FUCKING TALKING TO ME, RODNEY!" I yelled, stomping my way to his front door. Calling an Uber, I went home, and that was the last I'd heard from Rodney.

He didn't make sure I made it home.

He didn't apologize for being a fucking dweeb.

He just lived life and ignored me, as if nothing was happening. He was active on his social media, even more so than usual.

I didn't know what to do.

RODNEY

Yeah. We do need to talk. I'll swing by yo crib tn. Lmk when you make it in.

I POWERED my phone on and saw that Rodney had finally responded to my text.

The message was ominous. My stomach lurched, and I felt my mouth go dry. I finished my work day as best as I could, putting the finishing touches on the campaign that was going live. I had my birthday off and a few days next week off, and wondered if Rodney was surprising me with another trip this year. The year before, we went to Cancun. I wouldn't mind going somewhere tropical again.

Getting home, I quickly showered and changed into his favorite lounge set he liked to see me in; a silk short and camisole set in his favorite color of cobalt blue. Oiling myself in the new Zee Naturals body products and spraying perfume, I quickly poured us a glass of wine and got a quick dinner of jerk shrimp alfredo started. He told me that he was parking, so I took a glance at myself in the mirror. I was tired. Still feeling a bit sick, but not as bad as I was a few days before. I was ready to reconcile with my man, because these past few days of not speaking were trash.

He entered my apartment using the key I made him, and when he didn't greet me like her normally would – a kiss, followed by a grab or smack of my ass, I just *knew.*

Things had shifted between us.

He didn't even take off his shoes and declined the dinner and wine I had made.

We sat on my sectional – he in the armchair and me on the couch, clutching my glass of wine.

"So... I've had time to do a lot of thinking," he started. His voice was.... measured and void of emotion. My internal alarms were going off, and once again, I just *knew.* Instead of saying anything, I took a generous sip of wine and waited.

"It's no easy way to say this... and I don't want you to think it's all you.... But.... I think we should part ways, Saint. Shit just ain't the same between us no more." He met my eyes with his own, and I traced his features for any semblance of a joke. Trying to break up with me two days before my birthday was diabolical. Even the greatest of villainous niggas wouldn't pull no shit like this.

I gulped the rest of my wine down and set the glass on my table. Looking right at him, I narrowed my eyes.

"So let me get this straight... You totally ignore the fact that I wasn't feeling well, ask me to make food for you, call me selfish, ignore me for damn near three days, and then have the nerve to break up with me?"

I was in disbelief. I had never been broken up with before, so to say that I was shocked was an understatement. We've had disagreements. We've had moments where we've gotten on each other's fucking nerves. We've *never* gone days without talking to each other, though.

"You forgot to mention where you called me selfish and told me to get the fuck out yo face," he replied smugly.

My eyes bucked. "Because, nigga, *You were* being selfish! And incompetent like you don't know how to make salmon. You do, you just didn't want to. So perhaps... You earned that curse out?"

We held each other's stare, and the love that was usually in his eyes for me was replaced with guilt. Maybe even a bit of annoyance, because I wasn't making this easy for him. I had always heard that certain moments in your relationship would show you whether or not if the partnership was meant to last. And sadly, we weren't. Because if you couldn't be empathetic and kind to me when I was battling the common cold and seasonal depression, who's to say that you'd be kind and empathetic to me when I birthed children, or got laid off, or my seasonal depression became more permanent?

I could no longer ignore the red flags. Rodney and I weren't as perfect as we both tried to make it seem.

"Saint," he sighed. "Look, I'm sorry. But I also don't feel like our relationship style is aligned either anymore. You want traditional monogamy, and I don't want that. Isn't it better to cut our losses before we hate each other?"

"The thing is, I think you already hate me. Keep it a buck with me, Rodney. Is there someone else? Have you already started your ethical non-monogamy journey without my consent?" I sipped more of my wine with anger bubbling within me. If I were being honest, there were a lot of things that Rodney and I didn't align on; having a traditionally monogamous relationship was one of them. While I was perfectly fine with only fucking and being with him for the rest of my life, Rodney had more carnal desires. He was a wild boy in college, popular because he could rap, and naturally, women flocked to him. We started off as friends with benefits, and then when I caught strong feelings, I tried to break things off with him so he could be as free as he wanted, but he didn't take that news too well.

Crazy how I didn't know the difference between a nigga actually choosing you and a nigga being afraid to lose access to you back then.

Eventually, he propositioned me with a "let's try to date" agreement, and then he officially asked me to be his girlfriend six months later. About a year into our relationship, he asked what I thought about people who allowed others into their bedroom or those who had open relationships. I wasn't too passionate about it, so I didn't have many opinions, but I was clear in saying that's not what I wanted for myself.

Then he dropped a bomb on me, saying he actually did see that lifestyle for himself, and now I was in a conundrum. Do I leave my man that I love very much, or do I bear and grin while letting him sow his royal oats? Rodney figured that because I identify as bisexual, that meant that there would be threesomes galore. And while we did engage a couple of times, it wasn't something I wanted a lifetime of. I was just a woman who loved women. I wasn't bi for the aesthetics or the approval of men.

The thought repulsed me.

Rodney convinced me to stay, so I did. Now we were just a couple of months post our two-year anniversary, and here he was… breaking up with me. Hot tears gathered in my eyes, and I tried my best to hold it together. I hated losing control of my emotions, but my feelings were hurt.

"Saint. The truth may not be what you want to hear, but that doesn't negate it from being the truth… I didn't do anything without your consent, but I'd be lying if I said I didn't feel a shift between us… and I know you feel it too."

I said nothing as a tear broke out from my cell of emotions and rolled down my cheek. I didn't bother wiping them because I knew more were coming. Getting broken up with two days before your birthday, which also happens to fall on the same day where people celebrate love, is some villainous shit that not even Tyler Perry could come up with.

I wanted to yell, I wanted to throw shit, I even wanted to beg, but instead I was frozen.

"Saint? You not gone say nothing? You know I hate it when you cry, mama. We can still be friends," he made a futile attempt to comfort me. He crossed the threshold and tried to rub my shoulder, but I jerked myself from his touch. I felt him staring awkwardly at me, and then he stood. Rodney was never good with my tears, which is why I tried my best to conceal them. It's not that he lacked empathy, but what the fuck was I supposed to do with him awkwardly staring at me?

"GET OUT! GET THE FUCK OUT MY HOUSE!" I finally found my voice, and it was scorched with rage.

The nerve of this bean head ass nigga! I grabbed my empty vase since he didn't get me flowers this week and launched it at him, missing his head by half an inch. We both watched it hit the wall and shatter into pieces.

"Yo! You tweaking, man! Exactly why I don't wanna be with yo ass!" he spat. I jumped up from the couch, seeing red. Looking for the next thing I could throw at him, he turned on his heel and sped down my hallway and slammed my door.

"AND I WANT MY FUCKING KEY BACK!" I yelled to the void. I stared at the door for a minute, then found the nearest wall and slid down it, as if I was channeling my inner Summer Walker.

2

I didn't sleep last night. I almost called off work today, but decided not to since tomorrow was my birthday.

My birthday.

Who the fuck gets broken up with two days before their birthday?

As I tossed and turned all night, I swear I went through all the stages of grief. The anger and then the denial, as I destroyed my apartment. Broken glass was all over my living room floor, broken dishes littered my kitchen, and pictures were hanging lopsided on the wall. I thought about everything I'd given in this relationship. I sacrificed so many parts of myself trying to model patience, forgiveness, and acceptance, only to be broken up with two days before my birthday.

If I weren't so heartbroken, I'd laugh.

I sent that nigga seventeen text messages.

Cursing him out.

Begging him to come back.

Blocking him.

Then unblocking him.

Just to block him again.

Just to unblock him and profusely apologize.

Each one was left on read, so I felt even more shitty. I went through three bottles of wine, and it gave me a headache. I woke up this morning thinking last night was a dream, but when I looked at the tornado that was my crib, I knew that this was indeed reality.

Trudging to the bathroom, I almost shrieked at my appearance once I passed my cracked hallway mirror. I looked and felt like shit, yet I didn't have the luxury of tending to myself just yet. Shards of glass crunched beneath my house shoe-covered feet, and looking down at them almost made me throw up all the contents of my stomach. The house shoes I was wearing were a gift from Rodney a couple of Christmases ago.

Would I have to burn, throw away, and give away every stitch of clothing and shoes this nigga has ever given me?

I'd cross that bridge when I get there.

STARTING THE SHOWER, I put my mid-length locs in my bonnet and washed yesterday's makeup off my face. Like a zombie, I mechanically went through my five-step skincare routine and decided on pair of jeans, a long-sleeved red top, and red and white Dunks under my black peacoat. February weather in Chicago meant that it was cold, dreary, and snowing. I was hoping that me and Rodney would be able to get away and go somewhere warm. That's what we did the last couple of years for my birthday.

Walking into work, I noticed all the red and white decorations and remembered that we were doing our weekly wine down. Working in advertising meant that we worked hard and decompressed even harder. There was always a happy hour, a tasting, or a later dinner after work to tend to. I wasn't much of a hard liquor drinker, but today I would be. Walking over to my desk, I was greeted by the sight of balloons tied to my chair, a *Happy Birthday* streamer on the wall above my desk, and small red and white gift bags filled with Valentine's Day chocolates and some of my favorite candies.

Mustering up a weak smile, I turned to the growing group behind me and thanked them, then sat down to ideate some copy for another campaign.

"Still don't know what you're doing this weekend?" Jas asked, as we walked through our office building to grab a Red Bull and our usual for lunch.

I shook my head. "I wouldn't care if I just slept all weekend to be honest," I replied flatly. Jas's brows raised, and I prepared myself for the myriad of questions I knew she would ask.

"What is up with you? You seem so down today... birthday blues?"

I took a deep breath and shook my head. "Rodney broke up with me last night... we had a petty ass argument earlier in the week over me not cooking some salmon, I cursed him out and left the crib, and we didn't talk for damn near three days. When he finally did respond to me, he comes over to break up with me."

It sounded crazy to even say it out loud, but the truth was the truth.

Jas' jaw dropped. "HE BROKE UP WITH YOU? TWO DAYS BEFORE YOUR BIRTHDAY? THAT BITCH ASS NIGGA!" she shrieked, drawing attention to us.

"Keep your voice down, Jas!" I hissed. She lowered her voice but still expressed her disdain. "Oh Saint.... I just – this is just – are you okay? We can go slash that nigga's tires right now!"

My body stilled. *Was I okay?*

No.

Did I know I would eventually be okay?

The verdict was still pending on that.

What I did know was that I needed to make the best of my birthday weekend and not let impending heartbreak fuck me up.

How I was gonna pull it off is what stumped me.

SAINT

3

RODNEY:

Happy twenty-ninth birthday, Saint. Despite how you may feel, I do have love for you and wish that things were different between us so that we could spend today together.

I stared blankly at my phone, appalled at the audacity of Rodney's message. How do you wish that things were different between us when you were the one who ruined shit between us? I sucked my teeth, my feet hitting my heated hardwood floors as I trekked to my bathroom. This was the first birthday in years that I didn't have a plan for what I was doing or have anyone in particular that I was spending it with. Even back in college, Rodney and I shared some of the same friend groups, and with his birthday only eleven days after mine, February was always a busy and chaotic month for us both. As the hot water poured over my body, I began to laugh at the irony of it all. Once I got out of the shower and dried off, I decided to respond to his message.

Boy, fuck you.

All the shit we did together, went through, and overcame, and now I was reduced to text messages on my damn birthday. What's next? Not getting acknowledged at all on forthcoming birthdays? The thought made me want to weep.

Pull it together, Saint. Because Rodney may be a dickhead, but he didn't lie about the shift between ya'll. You felt it too. My inner voice was alive and awake, refusing to let me drown in delusion like me and Rodney were *so* perfect. We weren't. And that's okay.

But why do I feel so shitty?

Quickly dressing in a tan Hustle Honeyz jogging suit, I slipped on my boots and headed down the block to my favorite breakfast spot. It was barely noon, and they were already packed, but I knew the owner would save me a seat at the diner counter like she always did on my birthday.

SEEING ALL THE COUPLES, both young and old, canoodle together at their tables and booths almost made me turn my heartbroken ass right back around.

Maybe it was too soon.

"Saint! C'mere girl! You looking beautiful on your twenty-ninth birthday!" the owner, Sentury, called out. She was in her late thirties, queer, and owned this spot with her wife, Saturn. I'd been coming here on my birthday for years and even helped her with some website copy for the restaurant. Sentury always looked out for me and made a big deal out of my birthday. Even if I wasn't in the country, she and Saturn would always get me a gift and breakfast on the house when I got back.

I walked over to my reserved spot and gave Sentury a tight hug, and she lingered for a while, almost motherly like, and drew back and stared at my face for a few seconds.

"Saint. What's wrong?"

I shook my head, because I didn't wanna cry. Especially not on my birthday.

"No. Don't lie to me, or Imma call Saturn out here," Sentury crossed her arms and tapped her foot impatiently. I sighed. I knew if I talked to Saturn, I would really be crying because Saturn had this way of making you spill your guts whenever you were in her presence. People often just walked up to her and started telling her all their trauma.

She hated and loved it at the same time.

"I'll spare you the details but... Rodney and I are no longer together," I sighed. Sent's brows raised, and she tilted her head, studying me for a bit.

"Hmmm...." she said after a beat. "Well, I'm sorry to hear that because I know you're hurt behind it....you loved him. When did this happen?"

I bit the inside of my cheek, silently begging myself not to break down sobbing in the middle of this restaurant. "Two days ago," I mumbled. Sent's hazel eyes flashed angrily, and her jaw tightened.

"Two days before your birthday is crazy! I'm banning that nigga from my restaurant," she gritted lowly. I gave her the weakest smile, because Sent did not play. Rodney and I didn't come here together often, but he and Sent met a few times when we did. I could tell that Sentury didn't really care for him, and Saturn just straight up ignored him, saying that she didn't like his energy. In his words, Rodney just thought they were "two weird dyke bitches", but really, they just saw what I refused to see.

Rodney and I weren't aligned with each other. The relationship had plenty of good times and served its purpose for the time being, but the moment I realized that we didn't share the same values around our relationship styles, it should've been the day we parted ways amicably. Because if I want monogamy and you want to be ethically non-monogamous, then why are we still in a relationship?

Instead, we both held on, subconsciously hoping that one of us would change our minds, but it never happened. Instead, desires got buried, and instead of walking in truth and transparency, we just walked on eggshells with each other.

Over time, we started having surface-level conversations.

We had a mediocre sex life.

And we just went through the motions.

Saturn walked back in and set my plate of blackened catfish and grits down with a side of duck bacon and a peach mimosa. "Happy birthday, my girl. You wanna eat first or tell me who I gotta fuck up for trying to ruin your birthday?" she asked. I choked on my bacon, and she sighed while patting my back.

This bitch must be psychic.

"I keep telling y'all that I am not psychic... I just felt your energy when I walked in the room," she explained, reading my mind.

Me and Sent shared a laugh, and Saturn rolled her eyes. She sauntered to Sent's desk and perched on top of it, crossing her arms over her ample chest.

"Well, My World," Sent started. "Homeboy broke up with her two days ago."

Saturn's amber colored eyes flashed with agitation as she remained silent. I was busy stuffing my mouth with the catfish and temporarily forgetting my problems for the moment. Gulping down the rest of my mimosa, I stared at Saturn, silently asking her to go get me seconds. Their chef was from Louisiana, and it showed in the fried catfish they served daily.

"I'll be back, My Lifetime," Saturn turned and spoke to Saturn. I thought it was so cute that they called each other *My World* and *My Lifetime* based on their names.

Very lesbian coded if you asked me.

Saturn returned moments later with a full plate and two mimosas for me.

"Okay, Saint. I've had time to think about this –"

"More than me?" I teased.

Saturn shot me a playful warning glare. "Of course not. However, I know you're going through the motions. But you still deserve to have a good birthday," she looked to Sentury to chime in.

"We got you something... a massage at Aire Ancient Baths. And then, we can link up later tonight to go to The Promontory. They're having their Five Senses Party, and I think it'll be a good time. We reserved a section."

I wrinkled my nose. I enjoyed going to The Promontory, but I thought it was too soon to be going to places where Rodney co-existed. Like, it's one thing to get broken up with two days before your birthday, now I gotta risk bumping into the nigga in public too? I'll pass.

"I –"

"I know you think it's too soon, but you deserve to have a good birthday, Saint. I am so sorry that nigga tried to ruin it for you," Saturn continued with finality.

I stuffed a forkful of grits in my mouth and chewed on it, thinking of their proposition.

"Well, first of all... thank you for the gift. Secondly, what time should I be ready for this shindig?"

The couple smiled in unison. "Eight," Saturn replied.

"And my homie Rajani might be joining us too," Sent added.

We continued to chat well through the brunch hour, and then it was time for me to go to my massage appointment.

I had no idea how my evening would go, but if I was going to have a broken heart on my birthday, I would at least look and feel as best as I could.

4

One deep tissue massage, a loc retwist and style appointment, a nail appointment, and a deep clean of my apartment later, I was feeling.....

Kinda the same.

I wasn't a stranger to heartbreak, but this just felt heavier because of the history me and Rodney shared. Like, how do you just easily move forward from a nigga that you spent ten years of your life with? While only two of those years were spent in a relationship, our friendship bond was deeper than anything.

So I thought.

Unt uh bitch. Fuck him, it's yo birthday. Take a shot and then let Sent and Sat know you're ready, my inner voice spoke again.

I took one last look at myself and nodded in approval. Since the theme of the event we were going to was called The Five Senses, I dressed in a fire engine red, crushed velvet mini dress with matching tights, and my red Brandon Blackwood platform heels. The dress had a sweetheart neckline, so I had my girl Reina at Reigning Beauty touch up my honey blonde tips on my locs and put them in an intricate bun on the top with the back cascading down my spine. Rihanna's Ruby Woo lipstick adorned my lips, and I paired my makeup look with a smoky eye with red shadow on my water line and three coats of mascara since I didn't feel like being bothered with lashes tonight.

Click-clack.

Click-clack.

Click-clack.

My heels made the most noise in my otherwise quiet apartment as I made my way to the kitchen. The chilled Jon Basil bottle was waiting on me to pour myself a shot. As soon as I did, my phone rang to let me know that Sent and Sat were on their way upstairs. They looked cute in their matching red outfits, a two-piece suit set, and black fur coats. Sent's style was more androgynous, so while she didn't wear heels like Sat, she did have in her nose rings, five piercings in each ear, and gold rings on each finger with a red gloss that shone on her lips.

"You look gorgeous. These are for you," Saturn handed me a black satin-wrapped bouquet of roses with 'SAINT' spelled out in the middle, and my eyes watered.

My friends were thoughtful, but what about when my birthday was over, and I would miss getting flowers from someone every week?

"Unt uh! The only tears you are crying tonight are happy ones, babe. You can always buy yourself flowers, babe, you know that. And if we need to put together a flower budget together for you, then that's what we'll do," Sent grabbed me by the shoulder and stared me square in the eyes. I sniffled and nodded my head.

"Now give me this nasty ass shot so we can head out." I passed them both a shot and took another one with them. Their preferred vices were the occasional psychedelics and weed, so it meant a lot for them to indulge a bit with me. Grabbing my brown, knee-length fur, we headed down to my lobby to wait on the Xclusive Black Truck they rented for the night.

"To a good night!" Sent cheered, sipping on her flute of champagne.

"To a good night indeed," I declared, tossing my champagne back.

I just hoped I wouldn't regret it.

I HADN'T BEEN in The Promontory a full ten minutes, and I was already irritated and ready to go home. Don't get me wrong, I loved the spot because it was a true pillar of the community. You could come as you are, get a good drink, catch a dope show, and dance the night away if you wanted to. I was irritated because immediately as we walked in, I spotted Rodney at the bar, in not one, but *two* girls' faces. Skinning and grinning, as if he didn't try to ruin my life two days ago.

So much for wishing things were different between us.

You know how awkward it is to be in the same spot as your ex, fresh in your breakup, and they just seem... unaffected? After all the crashing out on his phone I did all week, I decided that I would channel my inner Meg Thee Stallion and Glorilla and pretend that nigga was dead.

Even if I was the one getting killed on the inside.

We made it over to our section, and their home girl, Rajani, was already situated with a couple more of their friends, seemingly all couples. I began to plot how I could skip this event early and just go home. In the morning, I'd probably book myself a quick flight to Puerto Rico and turn my phone off while I sat on the beach.

Rajani smiled at me, and I half-heartedly returned a smile, though I thought she was cute.

Nah... scratch that, shorty was *fine.*

She was about the same height as Rodney, a medium build with a nice ass, rocking a wavy Caesar cut with a beautiful smile. She was dressed in a black turtle neck, a Meaq chain, and flared red pants with a nice pair of black velvet dress shoes. Her mocha colored skin glistened under the red lights of the venue, and she smelled good, too, wearing a cologne I couldn't quite place but smelled of vanilla and mahogany teakwood.

Taking her in, I smiled at her for real, and she smiled back, with an intense stare locking in on me.

Is she flirting with me?

Yeah... she's definitely flirting.

It'd been so long since I'd been enamored with a woman. I wasn't blind, but I was indeed respectful of my relationship while I was in it.

"I hear that we got a birthday in the house," she smirked at me, letting me sit down in her spot. I nodded, unable to find my voice because she was just that fucking cute. We ended up making small talk, and I found out she was a year older than me and her birthday was eleven days after mine, just like... –

"Rajani? The fuck you doing here?" Rodney's voice cut through the music, and our heads popped up in confusion.

"Minding my fuckin' business, *bro*. Shouldn't you be somewhere wit yo girl?" she popped back. My eyes bounced in between them, and that's when it hit me.

Rodney. Rajani. Birthday is eleven days after mine. Are they –

"I'm here to collect her now," he sneered, looking at me. Rajani turned to me with a questioning look in her eyes, burning a hole in the side of my face.

What the fuck was this night turning into?

"Oh, this yo girl?" Rajani scoffed, leaning back and crossing her leg at the knee.

"No!"

"Yeah."

We both said at the same time, and I glared at him. Standing up slowly, I felt both Rajani and Rodney's eyes on me. Walking closer to Rodney, I jabbed my finger in the middle of his chest.

"Are you slow? Or does the liquor got you feeling froggy tonight? Nigga, you broke up with me two days before my birthday and then got the nerve to be in hoes' faces already. I'm not yours anymore, Rodney! You are free to do whatever the fuck you want, including getting the *fuck* out my face! Let me salvage what's left of my damn birthday, hell!"

Rodney's jaw dropped, and I spun on my heel to sit back down next to Rajani.

"Now, where were we?" I asked, pouring myself another cup of tequila and pineapple juice.

Rajani smirked at me, then watched Rodney tuck his tail and walk off from our section.

"You said bro broke up with you, huh?"

I stared blankly at her. "Bro who?"

She chuckled, tapping her middle finger to her thumb. "Ooop. Heard you, pretty lady. So then that means it's free rein to dance, then right?"

I smiled. Grabbing her hand, I led her to the middle of the dance floor, where plenty of other couples were jamming to the live cover of Janet Jackson's *Anytime, Any Place*.

My nerves were still a little frazzled, but the way our bodies sank into each other felt right. I closed my eyes, breathing in her scent deeply, and allowed myself to get lost in her touch. The thing I loved about women is that, regardless of how they presented themselves, most were really soft and gentle with their touch, which I appreciated. Softly, she caressed my lower back and asked if it was okay to touch me there. Once I gave my consent, she rubbed all over my waist and ass, while my hands circled her neck, and my cheek lay on her chest. Even with my heels on, she was a few inches taller than me. The live music ended, and the DJ came back on, switching the tempo up again by playing *Roster* by Jazmine Sullivan.

"If you could have anything for your birthday, what would you wish for?" Rajani asked in my ear. I shivered at her warm, minty breath tickling my eardrum.

"You a genie or something?"

She laughed. "If I was, you could def get three wishes. Ask away, pretty lady."

I licked my lips and looked at her. She stared at me intently, and I promised I almost melted.

"I wish I was getting kissed right now," I confessed boldly.

"Kissed where?" The question was loaded because the truth was, I wanted her to kiss me everywhere, and I hoped she was the kind who liked for a woman to return the favor.

I loved reciprocating.

"I'll leave that to your imagination. But for now, my lips." Rajani held my stare and pulled me closer to her, pressing her pillow-soft lips onto mine. In the middle of the club for all the people to see, we kissed like this was normal behavior for us, like two lovers sealing their infatuation for each other. I slipped my tongue in her mouth and tasted the mix of her mint and the liquor we both drank. Every nerve in my body had come alive, and if she wasn't holding me close, I would have fainted. Each time I tried to pull back, she chased my lips with her own, sucking on my tongue and bottom lip. Finally, she let us come up for air and broke the kiss. I now understand what the phrase "kissed stupid" meant.

"Two more wishes, pretty lady," Rajani said, wiping my smeared lipstick from the corners of my mouth with her thumb.

I smiled goofily, unable to find my voice again. Hand in hand, we walked back to our section, and she pulled me onto her lap. Sat and Sent were in their own world, canoodling on the other end of the couch like they always did when they had a chance to step out.

Turning sideways, I grabbed her face and pecked her lips two more times. "Kissing you is addictive," I confessed.

"I have to say the feeling is mutual," she kissed me again. "You gone tell me your next two wishes?"

"Mmmhmm. I'm still thinking," I breathed. "How about you tell me what you wish for?"

"But it's *yo* birthday, Saint."

I smirked. "Yeah, but.... Maybe I wanna give out a gift."

Rajani laughed again and kissed my forehead.

Girl. I'll laugh you right out yo turtleneck, don't play with me.

"Hmmm. I wish to make you feel good," she stared intently at me again, and my pussy thumped. Her hand was caressing my thigh, and I clenched my pussy muscles as if that was supposed to stop the pool of wetness gathering in the seat of my thong. Her fingers, long, soft, and well manicured with clear polish, inched closer and closer to my center, and at that point, I said fuck the kegels. My pussy was on the verge of leaking anyway.

Perhaps it would be a happy birthday indeed.

"Permission to take my fingers for a swim a lil bit?" she whispered in my ear and tugged at the waistband of my tights. I nodded my head profusely, closing my eyes in anticipation.

"I need your words, pretty lady. Use that pretty ass mouth and tell me I can take a dip real quick."

Popping my eyes open, I looked into hers and said, "Yes... You–you can take a dip real quick." My dress was bunched up around my hips, but nobody could see anything with the dimness of the club. Rajani dipped her finger inside my waistband, the soft pads of her fingers making contact with the smoothness of my mound. I shivered, but it wasn't cold in here. The girl barely touched me, and I was ready to cry out.

Leaning closer, she whispered in my ear, "Soft lips. Soft pussy. Thank you so much for letting me take a dip in your waters, Miss Mamas." Her middle finger circled my clit, and I opened my legs even wider, wishing I could snatch these tights off altogether. Grabbing her face again, I kissed her harder to drown out my moans while her finger dove deeper inside me.

"Ra-Rajaniiiii," I rasped, feeling my ending near.

"Wassup, pretty lady, you gone cum for me?"

My nipples hardened as I felt her go in and out of me, the combination of the lights, the liquor, and the lust taking over me.

It was okay to cum on your birthday, wasn't it? Even if the person making you cum was your ex-boyfriend's estranged twin sister?

"One more wish for the night, pretty lady... Can I have one more wish?" she asked, rubbing my clit again.

"Mmmmhmmmm, whatever you want," I moaned.

"Cum for me," and on command, I rained all on her fingers,

holding onto her for dear life with my face buried in her neck. When I was done, she slowly dislodged her fingers and licked them clean.

"Just as I expected. You taste good as fuck, pretty lady. How you feel?"

My brain was turning into mush, and I realized that the lights in the club were starting to come on. On wobbly legs, I slowly stood up and adjusted myself.

Hand in hand, we walked towards the exit and turned towards each other when we got to the bottom of the stairs.

"So –"

"Do you want to come home with me?" I blurted.

Rajani's eyes filled with lust. "Is that your final wish?"

I nodded.

"Good. Because my tongue wants to go for a swim too."

We called an Uber, and right as it was pulling up, we walked past Rodney, who was standing there looking shit faced, damn near foaming at the mouth, even with two women fawning over him.

I smirked to myself. I guess it was gonna be a good birthday after all.

The End

ACKNOWLEDGMENTS

Definitely need to take a moment to thank some people who brought this book to life.
Isatta, for your editing and proofreading prowess.
King Val, for your developmental feedback.
Jessica A., for being my pen sister and beta reader.
My Vibes and Lines crew, for supporting me!

Thank y'all.
Thank y'all.
Thank y'all.

Onward and upward we go.

KEEPING UP WITH KIA

Kia Smith is the author of moody, multifaceted musings about love. Hailing from the great city of Chicago and now based in Los Angeles, Kia brings heart and authenticity to each word she pens, leaving a lasting impression on readers long after they turn the page.

For more books, merch, and web exclusives, visit

www.kiasmithwrites.com

Join the Vibes And Lines Reading Group on Facebook here.

instagram.com/KiaSmithWrites
facebook.com/kween.k.smith
tiktok.com/@KiaSmithWrites
amazon.com/author/kiasmithwrites
threads.com/@KiaSmithWrites

ALSO BY KIA SMITH

Series

Love Rehab

Love Rehab 2

Non-Fiction

#WriteYourselfALoveLetterChallenge

www.ingramcontent.com/pod-product-compliance
Lightning Source LLC
Chambersburg PA
CBHW070628310726
48982CB00001B/198

9798993599021